THE
ILLUSTRIOUS
CLIENT

THE
ILLUSTRIOUS
CLIENT

SANDRA DE HELEN

For Miles, Maddy, and Courtney
for always asking me to read to you and to tell you stories.

ISBN 978-0-9910792-0-9

Contents

Cast of Characters   ix

Chapter One: Rose City   1

Chapter Two: Meet the Parents   5

Chapter Three: It's Xio Time   13

Chapter Four: A Little Acid Goes a Long Way   21

Chapter Five: Everything in Moderation   29

Chapter Six: Conversing   35

Chapter Seven: How Did This Happen?   41

Chapter Eight: Xio Times it Right   47

Chapter Nine: It Was Nothing   57

Chapter Ten: To the Morgue   65

Chapter Eleven: Accused Star to Be Arraigned   71

Chapter Twelve: A Night to Remember   81

Chapter Thirteen: First Date   91

Chapter Fourteen: In Other Words   101

Chapter Fifteen: My Girlfriend's Back   107

Chapter Sixteen: Second Chances   115

Chapter Seventeen: Afterglow   123

Chapter Eighteen: A Common Loon   133

Chapter Nineteen: Down and Out   141

Chapter Twenty: Wrap Party   153

Acknowledgments   157

What People Said about The Hounding   159

Coming Soon   160

Till Darkness Comes by Sandra de Helen   161

Chapter One: Seminal Event   163

CAST OF CHARACTERS

Shirley Combs, the world's greatest living detective (in her opinion)

Dr. Mary Watson, Shirley's best friend and sidekick, a naturopath

Lix, Combs and Watson's receptionist

Oceane Charles, a young international pop star, French

Therese and Austin Beaudet, Oceane's parents, French

Zaro Sadozai, about 40, wealthy Afghani woman who was raised as a boy

Bori Eszti, a rejected lover of Zaro's, Hungarian

Dody Pearce, a dead former lover of Zaro's, English

Elijah Reilly, Oceane's International Agent, from Portland, Oregon

Khalil Sadozai, Zaro's male cousin, Afghani

Beth Adams, Portland Realtor

CHAPTER ONE:
ROSE CITY

OCEANE LEANED HER HEAD AGAINST ZARO'S LEFT shoulder, laughing as she continued to sing a French lullaby to the giant panda she carried in her left arm. The night was cool as they strolled along Portland's waterfront away from the Rose Festival City Fair, and toward the privacy of Zaro's yacht. The bridge lights cast their rainbow colors on the water behind them as they passed the condos and strolled alongside the shop windows. Seagulls roosted on mooring pylons, letting her know it was probably later than she thought. She pulled her cashmere sweater a bit tighter as a breeze came off the Willamette River. Still, it wasn't raining as her friends had warned her it would do every day. Instead the days had been sunny more often than not for her visit to Rose City. She and Zaro enjoyed their relative anonymity here. Hardly anyone had recognized her as the European pop star she was. Not yet. Her performance would come on the last night of the festival, which meant she could remain relatively unknown and enjoy Portland as any other tourist would.

That was days ahead. Tonight they went to the carnival, rode rides, played games, and drank local wine.

As they approached the dock where Zaro's yacht, the *Freja*, waited for them, Oceane squealed a bit, and ran ahead. Zaro laughed and ran to join her. Together they raced up the stairs to the main level. Zaro's man Khalil opened the door and took their wraps, the stuffed bear, and asked what he could bring them. Zaro dismissed him for the night, and Khalil retired to his own quarters below decks. Zaro and Oceane hurried to the master suite, glancing at each other every few steps, smiling as if keeping a secret they could share with no one.

Zaro shut the door behind her. The king-size bed filled most of this quiet, lush cabin. The floor was overlain with Turkish rugs, the bed covered in silks and satins of grey and cream, with black, red, and orange pillows of various shapes and sizes. Oceane picked up the tiny remote and found a playlist of instrumental jazz to suit their mood. They met at the mirrored bar and Zaro poured wine for each of them from a bottle of Oceane's family's own vineyards. Tonight it was Chateau des Ouches's Special Selection, a sparkling white known as Cremant.

As the music played in the background, and the bubbly tickled their palates, Zaro and Oceane shed their clothes. Oceane chose a satin robe to match her eyes, the color of espresso. Zaro slipped into silk pajama pants. The pale ivory against her café au lait skin never failed to excite Oceane. She walked up to her and stood with her breasts against Zaro's as her fingers found the nape of her neck and felt her blue black mane. The short hairs on her nape were as soft as the plush on the panda she won for her at the carnival. She tilted her head up, gazing into Zaro's eyes, opening her lips, touching her tongue to her upper lip. With a groan, Zaro kissed her deeply, and lifted Oceane from the floor into her arms.

As Zaro gently lay Oceane onto the bed and pushed the pillows out of the way, Oceane never took her eyes off her. She couldn't believe this gorgeous woman was really hers. One of the most eligible lesbians in the world, with a fortune of her own, and bone structure any model would kill for—she knew Zaro had been with at least a hundred women before her. But ever since they met at the Rose Ball in Monaco, they were inseparable. That was nearly three months ago, and she had gone with her to every concert she had since. She had never had a woman cherish her the way Zaro did, cater to her every need or desire. She wasn't experienced like Zaro, of course. She was only twenty years old. She'd had boyfriends in high school, had even given up her virginity to one of them. And she dated women now and then since becoming so busy. But it was difficult to find anyone who was interested in her for herself in the music business, or so it seemed. They all wanted a piece of her—of her contracts, that is.

Zaro was different. She was protective and generous. She showed her love every day in ways big and small. She said she didn't care about her being famous, in fact she said she'd rather she weren't. She loved her voice, of course. It was what drew her to Oceane in the first place. She had asked Prince Albert and Princess Charlene to introduce them. But she would be happy if Oceane weren't famous, didn't have concerts booked, wasn't working on a new recording. To prove how generous she was in spite of all that, she had her yacht fitted with a recording studio so Oceane could work while they were abroad, and wouldn't have to leave at all.

Oceane touched Zaro's face, and gently pulled her head toward her own. Their mouths sought each other out, and their tongues played together as if they had minds of their own. When Zaro lifted her mouth from her, she slid under Oceane on the bed, and lifted her on top of her lithe body. She pulled her upright so she could tease her nipples, gently biting them through the robe, while cupping her behind with her hands. They both became aroused. Inside, Oceane felt a melting, a loosening of the muscles, a solid core of heat running from her breasts to her inner thighs. She wanted badly to pull down Zaro's pajamas and straddle her, but she let her take the lead as always. Zaro liked to keep her waiting until she was practically begging her to enter her. As she moved ever so slightly against Zaro's heated thigh, she moved her off, onto the bed. Zaro untied the belt of Oceane's robe, pulled it open, and began kissing her body. First the breasts, and under her arms and down to her wrists and hands, sucking a finger of each hand. And her neck, and down her chest to her flat belly, which she gave tiny licks. When she reached her pubic area she turned to her thighs and gave them bites as well as kisses.

Oceane was moaning with desire and ready for more when Zaro suddenly stopped what she was doing and sat up.

"What is it?" Oceane asked.

"Shh."

There was a sound outside the bedroom window. They both heard it this time. Zaro jumped up, threw back the drapes, opened the window and climbed out.

"Come back here, you!" She was actually chasing someone.

"Zaro, wait! Let me call the police. See, I'm calling them now." Oceane was dialing 911 on her cell phone when she heard Zaro scream. She climbed out the window, pulling at her robe with one hand, still holding the phone in the other. Khalil came running from somewhere, yelling "Stop her! Stop her!"

Khalil and Oceane reached Zaro at nearly the same minute. Zaro was screaming and writhing in pain. She couldn't tell them what had happened, but it was clear she'd been attacked. Khalil took the phone from Oceane and spoke with the emergency dispatcher asking for both police and an ambulance.

"It looks like acid."

CHAPTER TWO:
MEET THE PARENTS

S HIRLEY COMBS IS THE WORLD'S GREATEST LIVING DETEC-
tive. She says so herself. I agree, and happily assist her on her
cases, which I then document—sometimes in my blog DrMary-
Speaks, and sometimes in longer format, depending on the case. We
live and work in Portland, Oregon. Occasionally Shirley gets a case
which takes us out of town on business. This was one of those cases.
Or so we thought. Initially, Shirley received a phone call from Colonel James Damery. He was looking for the best possible help for his
friend's daughter, Oceane Charles, who had fallen for some scoundrel (Damery's antiquated term). The friend, Monsieur Beaudet and
his wife, Therese, ran a vineyard in the Loire Valley of France called
Chateau des Ouches, and rarely got away. They employed about fifty
people, but they were needed most of the year to oversee the work-
ings, the tastings, tours and so on. The daughter, Oceane, technically
grown at already twenty years old, was also a famous pop star in
Europe—but the parents were old-fashioned enough to believe they
could still influence her decisions regarding who she chose to marry
or partner.

Off we went to the Loire Valley to meet the parents. I had been
to Paris, but only for a week, when I first graduated from university
before I went to medical school. What I remembered best were the

Eiffel Tower, the Louvre, the wine and the cheeses. Shirley and I landed at the Charles de Gaulle International Airport at five in the afternoon, after being delayed in Warsaw for an extra hour and a half. We had been traveling since eight o'clock the previous morning, not counting the time we arrived at the airport. Thank the stars the Beaudet's were paying for business class airfare. Economy would have been too horrible. Especially as we went directly from the airport into the Beaudet's limo and drove straight to their Chateau through rush hour traffic, for another three hours.

When we arrived, shortly after eight, dinner was ready and waiting for us. All we had to do was freshen up and take our seats at the table in the immense dining room. Therese and Austin greeted us warmly and deferred speaking of business until after dessert. By then, we had sampled three of their wines, and I was feeling quite happy. Shirley was as solemn as always. I swear she has a hollow leg where alcohol goes to bypass her system. She never seems affected. Of course, she's taller than I am, and she did eat more bread, but could it really make that much difference? I'd have to ask her sometime. Meanwhile, I needed to sober up and take notes. I agreed to an espresso regardless of the hour. I was certain to be jet lagged in any case.

We adjourned to the library, where there was a stunning fireplace with an enormous tiled surround, fully functional as evidenced by the cozy blaze. Not too hot, exactly right in fact. We all made ourselves comfortable, and Austin began to speak.

"First I thank you for coming all this way to assist us in our problem Madame Combs."

"My pleasure, Monsieur."

"Second, my friend Colonel Damery speaks highly of your ability to solve cases, but I don't know if it will be enough to help us with our Oceane."

"I'm sure you're concerned."

Therese spoke up. "We're more than concerned. We don't know what to do."

I had to ask, "What have you tried so far?"

"We talked to our *avocats*, our how do you say, lawyers, of course," said M. Beaudet.

"What did they advise?"

"They said what we already know, Oceane is an adult and can do what she prefers."

"What do you hope I can do for you?"

"We want you to speak with Oceane, make her see she must leave this dangerous person."

Both Austin and Therese began to fill us in on the details. Oceane met Zaro Sadozai at the Rose Ball in Monaco in March when Oceane was one of the featured musical artists. She was introduced by the Prince and Princess at Zaro's request, and Zaro obtained this introduc-tion because she was a big donor to the Red Cross. She was a wealthy player, according to the Beaudets. She was disguised and raised as a boy in Afghanistan from the age of ten, and refused to resume the role of a young woman when she got old enough to marry. Instead she left home and made a fortune in investments. She chose to travel the world, date pretty young women, gamble, and make large char-itable donation.

Then came the darker side: Zaro was accused of murdering her companion a few years back, a young woman she had promised to marry. The evidence was all circumstantial, no DNA, no eyewitness. The girlfriends since the murder believed the story that she was set up. Framed. Apparently, Oceane was buying it as well.

"You want us to convince your daughter to leave Ms. Sadozai, because you believe she is a danger to your daughter." Shirley stated this rather than asked, but I knew what she was thinking because I was wondering the same thing. Were they trying to get her away from the woman only because she was a lesbian?

"Of course she's a danger," Austin said. "Besides, Zaro Sadozai is at least twice as old as Oceane. Old enough to be her mother."

"You obviously believe Zaro has some sort of hold over Oceane."

"Oceane says she is in love." Therese choked back a sob. "We raised our daughter correctly. If she were in her right mind, not under some powerful, hypnotic spell or dark persuasion, she would see using her talent is more important than a love affair. If the woman truly loved her she would support Oceane's career, not take her away from it."

"Where is Oceane now?" Shirley asked.

"She's on the yacht somewhere. We haven't spoken with her in weeks."

"Does she have another concert coming up soon? Will she cancel it?"

"She's never cancelled her concerts in her life. I'll have to check her calendar to see where she's going next."

"I have it here," said Austin, "she's in Portland, Oregon next Friday night, at something called Rose Festival."

"Back to Portland we go," said Shirley.

"No! You just got here, you must stay and tour the vineyards," said Therese.

"I'm sure Madame Combs knows what she's doing," said Austin.

"Mary, will you see when the next flight goes out?"

"According to this app, we can get on LOT at 7:30 tomorrow night. Everything before that is full."

"Even first class?" asked Austin.

"No, there's a flight at ten a.m. if we take the first class seats, but they're..."

"Never mind the expense. We can get you there on time. You had better retire now and get some rest."

"Before we retire, you should take this opportunity to tell us everything." Shirley was always practical.

"Ms. Combs is correct about discussing, Therese. We must use our time wisely. Still, we want you to fly first class so you can get back *tres vite*. Now, Ms. Combs, you know we are concerned about Oceane. This woman has a history of toying with young women's hearts. In fact, she killed one of her fiancées, and got away with it."

"How so?"

"She never went to trial, but everyone knows she did it. Like your O. J. Simpson."

"O. J. Simpson was found guilty in a civil trial. Was Zaro Sadozai?"

"I don't believe there was a trial of any kind."

"What does Oceane say about the killing?"

"She says Zaro didn't do it, and we are trying to persecute her."

"I will look into it."

"There are so many other young women in Zaro's past. I believe some of them have stalked her."

"That doesn't deter Oceane?"

"Nothing has deterred her so far. We are hoping you will."

"We will."

"How can you be so certain, Ms. Combs? My husband and I tried our best with our daughter, and she seemed so hopelessly in love."

"We will find the key, I swear to you."

Shirley spent another hour assuring the couple. She did this by recounting some of her most difficult cases, and her methods of solving them. The Beaudets were as astounded as most people were. Shirley saw things no one else thought to look for. She took the most minute items of data and put them together as if they were puzzle pieces until the cases fell together into a picture anyone could recognize. I was becoming accustomed to the ease with which she did this, but I was no closer to doing it myself. As she so often told me, I saw, but I did not observe.

When we finally went to our rooms for the night, there was little reason to unpack even my carry-on for what amounted to about three hours of shuteye. So much for touring the Loire Valley. It was dark when we arrived, and just starting to get daylight when we sped away. I saw some green fields, some trees, some vineyards, and birds I couldn't identify at the speed we traveled. The airport was okay. They treated us well in spite of our nationality, and they had great coffee. The Frederic Chopin Airport in Warsaw had a decent VIP Lounge in Terminal A where we spent a lot of time using Wi-Fi, catching up on e-mail. I surfed the web, played with my apps, and managed to keep my eyes open until we got on the plane for Chicago. I took full advantage of first class treatment: pillow, blanket, flat-down seat, and slept all the way to O'Hare.

In Chicago, we saw the news. Zaro Sadozai had been the victim of an acid attack. She was now at Oregon Health Sciences University Hospital where she was in critical condition. No one had been arrested in conjunction with the attack.

Shirley called her contacts at Portland Police Bureau before we boarded our last flight to learn what she could about what was known so far. I called my friends and asked for all the the gossip.

We boarded the flight and began to prepare for our landing by reading every article, going over every e-mail message, reading all the background we could find on Zaro and Oceane. Shirley knew a lot about the different types of acid that might have been used in the attack, and made the deduction—based on what was being reported regarding Zaro's injuries—the perpetrator had used hydrochloric acid at a close range. Given that, she further deduced Zaro might regain her eyesight with proper treatment. We would know more once we learned how quickly Zaro had been treated, how badly her eyes were burned, whether the doctors used the correct treatment for the acid. And even whether the acid were indeed hydrochloric. There were other possibilities.

This case had started out as one thing and now so quickly had morphed into something else. First we were flying across the world to an estate in France where I looked forward to meeting the parents of a celebrity, and to trying out my few French phrases. I knew it was shallow of me to be excited about meeting a pop star young enough to be my daughter, but I'd never met one before. A pop star, that is. What would she be like? A diva? Lounging around demanding "sweets" and champagne? Not getting up before midday or later? Maybe addicted to drugs? Or would she be a professional singer who was taking care of her voice, practicing her repertoire, recording at odd hours?

One thing for sure, she was self-assured at the age of twenty. Earning her own living, in love with a woman twice her age, sailing around the world on a yacht, performing for royalty. Who wouldn't want to meet her? A person wouldn't have to be shallow to want to meet someone like that. No, she must be fascinating. And now, she was alone in a strange city, a strange country, her lover wounded, in the hospital. She might be in danger. I wondered if the Portland Police Bureau was protecting Oceane. Her parents hadn't said anything about her traveling with bodyguards the way some pop stars did. Why didn't we think to ask? Shirley was napping, or I'd have asked her.

What about Zaro Sadozai? What made her so irresistible? I did an internet search on Zaro and came up with fourteen pages of links by using not only Google and Bing, but older search engines like Dogpile. Many of them had to be translated in order for me to read them. There were images of her and her yacht, links to articles about her trial, her former girlfriends, links to Oceane's links, over thirty-five hundred articles in all. I learned that Sadozai is a Pashtun tribe, traditionally considered to descend from Sado Khan. I wasn't sure what that meant, so I decided I'd better study. I found that apparently, Sado Khan was the lord of the Afghans, but the Sadozai could be Pakistani, Persian, or even Indian from Kashmir, according to Wikipedia.

Zaro herself took a good picture, even the paparazzi shots showed great bone structure, fine features, white teeth. Her history spoke to her charm. Or maybe it was her style, social class, and money. In any case, she kept company with the illustrious set. I wondered if one of them threw the acid, or whether it was someone new in her life. Could she be already cheating on Oceane? I couldn't speculate with Shirley. She never participated in those games. She'd rather I didn't either, but I didn't see the harm. I saw it as brainstorming.

It wasn't as though I was rushing out to put handcuffs on anyone based on my random thoughts. Shirley was a private investigator. I was her assistant. Still, I was a doctor. So, when I interviewed clients, I introduced myself as Dr. Watson. Sometimes they were confused as to why they are being interviewed by a doctor, but Zaro wouldn't be. I could be helpful to her in more ways than one. I could hardly wait to meet her.

CHAPTER THREE:
IT'S XIO TIME

IN FOUR DAYS WE SPENT SIXTY-SIX HOURS GETTING TO AND from Paris, six hours driving from Paris to the Loire Valley and back to the airport, four hours pre-boarding (two on each end), and no minutes retrieving our bags when we got in to PDX airport. Shirley and I dashed out the front entrance, ran across to the taxi stands, hopped in the first available and rushed off to our offices in downtown Portland in the Bank of America Financial Center on the 19th floor. It was barely noon, so getting an elevator was another delay, but at least we had great reception for our mobile devices. Shirley used her iPad to check her calendar, and I glanced at the few dozen e-mail messages that had come in to the business while we were in-flight. Most were from my list serves or fans of my blog, but two stood out: one from M. Beaudet and one from Colonel Damery.

I forwarded those to Shirley and simultaneously told her I was doing so, but not from whom as we were in public. As we stepped off the elevator onto the 19th floor, Lix, our receptionist was about to step on, apparently going to lunch.

"Lix, do you mind waiting a bit for lunch?" I could see she did mind, but she said no, and turned around and led the way to our offices on the east side. We moved into this building last fall after the first case we did for Colonel Damery. He brought in a consult that resulted in a decent fee and a massive bonus. Shirley decided it was time for us to join forces publicly. Now both our names are on the door. She still does some financial consulting, and I still do medical work in my field as a naturopath, but our primary work relates to her engagements in detecting. Colonel Damery's friends are mostly European and rich beyond anything we are accustomed to seeing here in Portland. There may be people in the Great Northwest who have that kind of wealth, but if so, they hide it. The friends to whom we've been introduced have mansions, yachts, villas, riding stables, vineyards, even private islands. I've seen things since working with Shirley that I had only previously read about—both bad and good.

Our offices are only a few blocks from Shirley's previous office. I once dreamed of working in Oregon City and overlooking the waterfall. But as it turned out the office in which I'd had that fantasy belonged to a murderer, and I lost interest. Besides, we are close to City Hall here, and that comes in handy. We're also near the Justice Center where the jail is located. Sometimes Shirley has to interview citizens who are locked up. This was one of those days.

Both Colonel Damery and M. Beaudet were e-mailing about the attack on Zaro, of course. They wanted Shirley to find out everything she could and inform them immediately. Both were offering to pay for anything she would relay.

Shirley contacted the Portland Police Bureau and spoke with Lt. Xio (pronounced "show"), head of the Person Crimes Division. This division has details for homicide, assault/bias, robbery, and sexual assault. Lt. Xio is the man in the know for all of them, and he assigns whichever detectives he thinks is the right one for the job, no matter which detail she or he is slotted into. Xio is Shirley's Lestrade. He is always willing to take the credit for crimes solved, and not always quite so willing to share information. Shirley has her ways. And she has me. When Xio isn't as forthcoming as we need him to be, I have friends in the PPB who will usually come through. We have to be absolutely discreet, and we have to be within the law. I've found free healthcare to be a good incentive, even for people with benefits provided by the city. Hardly anyone provides free naturopathy, and everyone can benefit from it. When western medicine was called for, I referred my patients to their primary care physicians. When a person had a cold or a virus, the cramps, or needs to be well and truly heard—there was nothing like an hour with a naturopath. I knew exactly what to do and how to make a person feel better.

Xio told Shirley that the PPB's primary suspect in the acid incident was Borbála (Bori) Eszti of Bana, Hungary. She is a former companion of Zaro Sadozai. They have an eyewitness, Khalil Sadozai, Zaro's valet/cousin. He saw Bori running away, and yelled for crew members of Zaro's yacht to stop her. They did, and held her until the police arrived. Zaro was Life-Flighted to OHSU directly from her yacht, which had its own heliport. She had two helicopters of her own, but neither was equipped for medical emergencies. Shirley requested permission to interview Ms. Eszti. Lt. Xio asked who Shirley's client was, and she replied that she was not at liberty to say. As usual. Xio granted permission, knowing full well that Shirley would learn something he wouldn't or couldn't, and that if it helped his investigation, she would share it with him. I went along to take notes.

Once we had everything squared away in the office, we sent our assistant Lix back to the airport to retrieve the bags, bring them to the office, and take the rest of the day off. We could handle everything else electronically until tomorrow.

At the Justice Center, we were allowed to interview Ms. Eszti in an interrogation room. Not everyone had this privilege, but Shirley was well-respected here. For the time being. We didn't like to take anything for granted. Police departments can be political, and the PPB was no exception. We had a new mayor, and who knew what the future held?

A uniformed corrections officer brought Ms. Eszti in and handcuffed her to the table. He walked out of the room and shut the door. We knew he would return at the touch of a button, should the prisoner prove violent. Or when we were finished with our interview, whichever came first. I didn't expect violence, but is one ever truly expecting it when it does arise? Not in the case of this woman, surely. She entered the room quietly, head down, hair limp and unwashed. She was here without her usual hair products, and evidently had chosen to do without rather than use the jail's plain shampoo. She wore no makeup, and was dressed in PPB's uniform of white tee shirt, cotton pants, white socks and flip flops, standard issue for men and women alike. The pictures I saw of her on the Internet looked like Uma Thurman. Now she looked like a stand-in for Goldie Hawn in *Death Becomes Her.*

"Ms. Eszti, I'm Shirley Combs, and this is my assistant Dr. Mary Watson. We'd like to speak with you about the incident the night of June 8 if you're willing."

"Did my attorney send you?"

"No. Who is your attorney?"

"My father hired someone. I haven't met her yet. She is from Portland. I am not."

"If I'm not mistaken, you're from near the Austrian border of Hungary."

"How do you know this?"

"Your accent."

"My English is excellent, I'm told that all the time."

"Shirley is very good at knowing where people come from, Ms. . . . ."

"Call me Bori, please. I don't like to be so formal, especially with other women."

"Very well, Bori. Please tell us what happened on the evening of June 8."

I was taking everything down, of course. But I was especially eager to hear the answer to this question of Shirley's.

"I've already told the police all I'm going to say."

"We aren't the police, Bori. I'm a private investigator."

"Are you here to help me?"

"I'm here to learn the truth. I don't know yet whether that will help you."

"Someone threw acid, it landed on Zaro Sadozai, and the police arrested me. I've been indicted on suspicion of attempted murder. That is what happened."

"Did you throw the acid?"

"Zaro is a horrible woman. She killed her fiancée and she ruined my life as well. Now she's going to ruin Oceane Charles's life." She put her head on the table and began to sob.

"Tell me about Zaro."

"I told you. She's terrible."

"You said she killed her lover. Why isn't she in prison?"

We knew very well why she wasn't in prison. The woman's death was proclaimed accidental, and all evidence was circumstantial. No charges were ever filed. Not only not against Zaro, but not against anyone. Was Bori a jealous lover gone mad?

"She told me she had enemies who tried to frame her for Dody's death. That it was an accident. She didn't do anything wrong. She would never hurt a beautiful woman, in fact she wouldn't hurt anyone. I was so in love with her I believed everything she said. That's what happens: young women fall for her and she gets away with murder!"

"How did she ruin your life, Bori? Did she hurt you physically?"

"She broke my heart. And when I tried to talk to her, to reason with her, she accused me of stalking. She had me arrested."

"So you sought revenge?"

"I tried and tried to talk to her."

"You followed her all over the globe?"

"Of course not. I was here in the States for a Lipizzaner show and sale of one of our mares."

"Here in Portland? Because the only Lipizzaner show I know of took place in New York City over a week ago."

"Yes, that was the one." Bori was one of those people who makes me jittery because she was never still. She tapped her fingers on the table, she jiggled her feet, or bounced her knee. It was going to be hard to know when she was telling the truth.

"You came here after."

Not a question. Shirley was leading Bori step by step.

"Obviously." Tap tap.

"How did you travel?"

"I drove." Jiggling her feet all the way?

"You have an international driver's license?"

"Of course."

"Which rental agency did you use?"

"I borrowed a car from a friend."

"A trusting friend."

"Yes."

"Where is the car now?"

"I can't say." She taps out a morse code signal on the table.

"Can't or won't?"

"Can't."

"I see."

I looked at Shirley. How did she know what Bori meant by "can't" in this instance? I knew Shirley meant she fully understood Bori, but I certainly didn't. I made a note to ask after the interview.

"What is the make and year of the car?"

"I'd rather not say." A baby on her knee would fall off.

"Moving on. Where are you staying in Portland?"

"At the River Place condos. I'm couch surfing."

I couldn't help interrupting. "I always wanted to try that myself. Did you find the place online?"

Both Bori and Shirley stared at me. They continued as if I had burped without excusing myself.

"So you are staying near Zaro's yacht."

"I was until I was arrested."

"You were watching her."

"I wasn't stalking her."

"You observed her?"

"I saw her and Oceane a couple of times."

"Did they see you?"

"I don't know."

"You know they didn't. If they had, you would have been arrested."

"Probably."

"When did you see them?"

"They were walking by the condo. I was looking out the window."

"With binoculars?"

"No. I could see them plainly. They were right below me. I was on the second floor facing the water front." I doubted she could hold binoculars still.

"Where were you at the time of the attack?"

"What time was that?'"

"Evening. Say the hours between seven and eleven."

"I spent all evening indoors. I was on the couch in the condo, reading." Reading what? Pop-up books?

"Any witnesses?"

"No. The owners are at my home in Bana. We exchanged."

"Where did you get the acid, Bori?"

"Officer! I'm ready now, please."

The officer must have heard her call, because he peeked in the glass window of the door. She waved him in.

"You have motive, you had opportunity, and you certainly knew how to obtain the means. Once the police find out you obtained the acid..."

"Goodbye, Miss Combs. It was nice speaking with you. Next time, please speak with my attorney instead."

I could feel Shirley's frustration, even though she hadn't changed her demeanor. I didn't know what our next step would be. I was pretty certain Bori had thrown the acid. I was surprised she hadn't splashed it on herself in the process. Maybe a jury would find reasonable doubt based on her inability to hold still long enough to complete the process.

CHAPTER FOUR:
A LITTLE ACID
GOES A LONG WAY

SHIRLEY PUT LIX TO WORK ON CONFIRMING HOW BORI GOT from New York to Portland, compiling a complete and detailed itinerary, down to the minute, and with copies of receipts attached. I wasn't needed for this task because I was called to consult on Zaro's medical case. One of my dearest friends in Western Medicine, Dr. Ellen Jepperson, worked at OHSU up on so-called Pill Hill, and she was heading up the team assigned to look after Zaro Sadozai. Zaro was in a luxurious VIP room reserved for the rich and/ or famous. She was, of course, receiving the best of care the Oregon Health and Sciences University had to offer. They had no intention of losing this patient to one of the other hospitals. OHSU snagged her because they were the closest trauma unit to where her yacht was docked. To keep her, once her condition stabilized, they also had to be sure she was happy with her care. So they decided to supplement the luxurious room and fabulous view with acupuncture, massage, and naturopathy. That's where I came in.

I put on my best consulting outfit and a lab coat fresh from the cleaners. Picked up my doctor bag, small purse with the cross-body strap for wallet, keys, and sunglasses, and headed out the door. Parking on the hill can be a nightmare, even for visiting consultants, so I parked down on the south riverfront and took the tram. Portland's tram offered the best view of the city, also of Mt. Hood, Mt. St. Helens, and the river with all its bridges. It was a short ride, but absolutely delightful.

Zaro didn't need to ride anywhere for her view. Her floor to ceiling wall of windows looked out directly on Mt. Hood. Unfortunately, she couldn't see it, as her upper face and head were covered in bandages. The sun shone in the windows making clear the damage done to her once handsome features, even though they were covered. There was seepage. Also, her mouth showed signs of stress as she clenched and loosened her jaw. Someone had micro-shaved her chin this morning, but they hadn't done the job she was accustomed to. She kept picking at a minuscule patch of missed stubble. Oceane sat in a chair pulled up to her bedside. She stood up as I came in.

"Good morning, Ms. Sadozai. I'm Dr. Mary Watson, a naturopathic physician. I'm here to consult on your case."

"Good day, doctor. This is my, this is Oceane Charles." Zaro had a slight middle Eastern accent, impeccable English, probably the second of many of the languages in which she was fluent.

I turned to Oceane. "I'm pleased to meet you, Mademoiselle Charles, but I'm going to have to ask you to leave us alone while I examine the patient."

She left. Not without a huff and a backward glance. She didn't go far. Through the wide glass panel next to the room's entrance, I could see her lurking right outside the door.

"Sorry to run off your company."

"That's fine. What exactly is a naturopathic physician? I'm not familiar."

"We practice medicine that is based on the belief that the human body has an innate healing ability. We treat people as whole beings, not as their injuries or symptoms, or illnesses. Our treatment plans blend the best of modern medical science and traditional natural medical approaches to not only treat what's wrong, but to restore health."

"You're going to give me herbs and tinctures?"

"First things first, please."

"What's first?"

"What we naturopathic doctors like to do first is ask lots of questions, get to know our patients. Do you mind if I sit down?"

"No, okay. I didn't know you were still standing." Zaro wriggled around on the bed, making herself comfortable for a longer conversation.

"Are you okay? Do you need anything before we begin?"

"No. I have my morphine button right here." She pushed it. And she took a swig of water from her water bottle.

"Let's get started before you need to doze. I'm going to begin by taking a sort of brief health history, Zaro, may I call you Zaro?"

"Sure, if I can call you Mary." This one was a charmer. Did I want her to call me Mary? Hm.

"Let's keep it formal, Ms. Sadozai. Tell me about your injury."

"Bori shot acid in my face with a water pistol. I thought you knew that."

"You saw her with the acid?"

"No, but I know it was her. I smelled her perfume. And besides, she's the one who's been stalking me."

"Did you see the water pistol?"

"No, the police told me that's what it was. They found it on the dock."

"Tell me about the injury itself."

"Hurts like everything."

"Can you give me a number on a pain scale? If zero is no pain and ten is the worst you ever felt, where is the pain right now?"

"Right now? I'd say about a seven."

"What about when it happened?"

"Definitely a ten. More if that's possible. I can't even describe what it felt like. I couldn't stop screaming. I want to kill her for hurting me so bad."

"Is there anything that makes the pain better?"

"Morphine."

"Anything make it worse?"

"Touching the place where the acid burned my skin off. Thinking about whether or not I'll ever see again. Trying to cry and not having tears."

"I understand. And what do you do when the pain is worse?"

"Push this button."

"Do you feel like the pain is getting better day by day?"

"Not yet I don't."

"Do you feel like it's getting worse or staying the same?"

"Same."

"Who all have you seen for the problem and what has the treatment been?"

"Can't you just look at my chart?"

"Ms. Sadozai, I have looked at your chart. The reason I ask these questions is also for me to see what your understanding of your injury and treatment are."

"Ok. Dr. Ellen, of course. She's the main one. And there's Dr. Carruth, the Chinese medicine guy who does acupuncture and other treatments. And Dr. Svelak from Los Angeles is coming up to see me about doing plastic surgery when I'm ready for it. I'll go down there to have it, of course. I can recuperate on my boat."

"What did Dr. Ellen do for you?"

"The EMTs got to me first, and flooded me with water before they put me in the helicopter to transport me up here. By that time I was unconscious, but they gave me oxygen and so on. Up here Dr. Ellen treated the burns, my respiratory system, treated me for shock, and for pain."

"I'm going to ask you a series of questions. Please answer quickly, without thinking. But first, what is your current stress level, again on a level of one to ten, with ten being highest."

"Six."

"Good. Now, remember. Answer true or false right away. We'll keep going."

"Fine."

"True or false: Appetite at breakfast is strong."

"False."

"You crave salt."

"True."

"Fruits generally do not agree with me."

"False."

"Your ear color is red or pink."

"True?"

"Your skin tends toward oil and moist."

"True."

"Your hands and feet are warm."

"True."

"You urinate large volumes daily."

"False."

"You often need to urinate during the day."

"True."

"You react poorly to criticism."

"What does this have to do with anything?"

"Please, true or false only, and quickly."

"False."

"You are bothered by confrontation."

"Fuck this. What the hell?"

"These are routine questions. If you didn't have bandages on, you could simple fill out the form, circling true or false. There are three sections, forty-nine questions in all."

"I'm finished."

"I won't be able to make an accurate assessment with so little information, Zaro."

"Do the best you can based on the fact that I piss a lot, don't wake up starving, and get fed up with stupid questions from irritating doctors."

"You're stressed and having a lot of pain. Morphine will handle some of the pain, but it will also cause constipation. You will need to drink a lot of water, walk as much as possible, and I'd like to prescribe yoga exercises for both relaxation and to aid in digestion. I can order meals to help as well. Do you have any special dietary requirements?"

"Do you mean religious?"

"Any at all, gluten-free, vegetarian, allergies?"

"I prefer a Mediterranean diet with fresh organic vegetables, fresh cheeses rather than aged, and whole goats milk yogurt. I'd like some dates. Can you get those things for me?"

"I can not only get them, I can prescribe them. Anything else?"

"What about medical marijuana?"

"No. Do you use it?"

"No. I thought I'd ask. Are there alternatives to morphine?"

"None that are going to provide the level of pain relief you will need for the next few days. I'm glad you're asking. I'll speak with your other doctors."

"Maybe I could have some dates and goat cheese now?"

"Yes, I'll have some sent to you right away. We can continue this interview the next time I see you. For now I'm prescribing a homeopathic medicine to help your body start the healing process. The nurses will see that you are dosed on time and appropriately. I'll send a yoga instructor to teach you the moves to aid in your digestion."

I made sure she was settled, her water and nurse bell were in easy reach, and made my way out. Oceane re-entered the room the instant I left it.

As I sat in the tram looking out at the city, I reflected on my patient. The woman might be a killer, but it was impossible not to feel compassion for the person in the hospital bed who might never see again, and who would likely have difficulty breathing for the rest of her life from the damage done by an ounce or two of hydrochloric acid delivered by a water pistol. I texted Yoga Central to send their best instructor out to teach her how to do a few Asanas. Dahn called me back to confirm and assured me Zaro would receive VIP treatment and complete confidentiality.

In my car on the way back to the office, I listened to a culture program on KBOO. Dmae Roberts was interviewing a woman Taiko drummer about a concert they were doing for Rose Festival. There were so many programs going on during the festival. Portland was filled with tourists as well as artists, musicians, and sailors at this time of year.

At the office, I made up a patient file for Zaro, entering as much information for her as I could from her OHSU files, and what little I'd learned from our conversation. If she were an actual patient, rather than a consult, there were lots of ways to help her begin to heal her body. In my opinion she had probably never dealt with her gender dysphoria, and I would have loved to discuss it with her. Maybe dysphoria was too strong a word. Her history of having lived as a boy in her home country would be interesting to anyone who hadn't lived it. I wondered whether she ever talked about it? And there was the fact she had refused to return to "normal" life as a girl after living as a boy all those years. According to the articles I'd read, she'd been tossed out of her family for refusing to marry a man, had found success as an investor, and made her way without their help. She wasn't living as a man, but she wasn't living as a traditional woman either. She chose a fast life, fast cars, gambling, and young feminine women as her companions. So far she hadn't married, but she had been engaged at least once, maybe more than once. And now someone had attempted to kill her.

I knew it was our job to steer Oceane away from Zaro, and certainly I didn't want to see Oceane in danger. I did however have a strong desire to spend more time with Zaro. I wanted to know more about her past, more about her psyche, and why other women found her attractive. Maybe it was her eyes. I hadn't seen her eyes. From what I read in her chart, there was damage to the eyelids, and current loss of vision in both eyes, as well as damage to her nose, and a great deal of facial tissue. Apparently, they had gotten to her quickly enough with enough water to avoid the deep burns that happen otherwise. And the fact that the perpetrator used a squirt gun kept the acid from splashing widely. Zaro might regain her sight, and the fact she could afford the best plastic surgeons meant she would be able to restore her good looks.

I shook myself. Zaro didn't need my sympathy. Oceane needed my help in removing herself from Zaro's spell. Whatever hold Zaro had on Oceane, it could be broken, and it was Shirley's and my job to break it. Shirley would use her logic. I would study my Bach's Flower Remedies to see if I could find something to help us. A few simple pellets under Oceane's tongue several times a day in the guise of helping her (to what? Stay awake?) might turn her focus away long enough for us to capture her attention. It was worth a try.

CHAPTER FIVE:
EVERYTHING IN MODERATION

S HIRLEY CALLED ME FROM FAT CITY, ONE OF OUR FAVORITE
breakfast hangouts. It was located in Multnomah Village about
halfway between my small place in Lake Oswego and OHSU where
Zaro was ensconced and Oceane was never leaving her side. When I
arrived, the secondhand was sweeping seven on the dot and Shirley
was sipping her coffee, looking at me over the rim of her mug. No
plates were on the table, so at least she hadn't started eating without
me. Fat City was just around the block from Marco's where we often
go, but FC has gravy. I thought gravy was something people ate only
at Thanksgiving unless they were, well, unhealthy. But all it is really
is a bit of fat, a bit of flour, and a bit of liquid. At home I made mine
with olive oil, nutritional yeast (instead of flour), a splash of tamari,
and water or veggie broth. At FC they used butter or sausage drip-
pings, flour and milk. Still a couple of tablespoons won't kill you if
you have it only once a week or so. Everything in moderation, that
was my new motto.

Shirley didn't have a food motto that I could discern. She seemed
to take in just enough fuel to keep her going, and not much care
what it was. One of my jobs as her naturopathic friend was to put
healthy options in her way. Therefore that day, I ordered brown rice,
poached eggs, and a large fruit salad plate. I knew she would pick

the berries from my plate if I placed it between us, and berries were good for one's brain.

Over our meal, I told Shirley about my research into the flower remedies. I'd found something I thought might help us, but it would take a few days to work, and only if Oceane took the pellets as prescribed. We were going to begin talking with Oceane today, but we didn't know how long it would take us to complete our mission, so I would try to get Oceane to agree to take the pellets.

After breakfast, I left my new Smart Car parked on the street, and we took Shirley's Mercedes up Terwilliger the back way to OHSU. Typical June morning, overcast and cool, a bit misty, especially up there in the hills. People were arriving for work as we pulled into the visitors' garage and began circling, looking for a parking space. These were the people who ran the offices, managed the clinics, worked in the pharmacy. Nurses and doctors were on different shifts, ten or twelve hours, starting at ungodly hours that gave them un-rush hours and more stress hormones shooting through their veins.

Because I visited Zaro the day before, we knew exactly where to go to find Oceane. When we arrived at the VIP room, there were no carts standing in the halls, no noise from other patients, nothing like a usual hospital experience—so long as we remained outside her door. Shirley rapped sharply. Within a couple of seconds, Oceane, opened the door just a sliver and whispered "she's sleeping."

"We're here to see you, Ms. Charles."

"Oh." She looked back into the room, pulled her sweater around her body as if she were leaving to go outdoors, stepped into the hall, and agreed to see us.

We all stood there for a few seconds.

"Ms. Charles, do you want to come to my office, or shall we go to the cafeteria here at the hospital to talk?" Shirley liked to give her clients options. But not too many.

"There's a private conference room down the way. Let me ask the head nurse."

Oceane walked several yards to another room, opened the door, stepped inside for a moment, and came back with a plastic card key. We followed her to a private conference room that would hold at least twenty people, but its view was of the road that continued to wind up the hill, not the mountains the VIPs got to see. Presumably this would keep the doctors, nurses, and consultants' minds on their business as they discussed cases.

Shirley could keep focus while being dragged by wild horses and shot at by deranged marksmen, I'm pretty sure. I'm wasn't quite that concentrated. I was working on it.

"Thank you, Ms. Charles."

"Please, call me Oceane."

"Very well, Oceane, I'm Shirley Combs, Private Investigator, and this is Dr. Mary Watson. We're here to ask you some questions about the acid incident the other night."

"Oh! I thought you were here about Zaro's condition. You were here just yesterday doctor, why have you brought an investigator?"

"I'm sorry…" I began.

"Sorry for the confusion, Oceane," said Shirley, "Dr. Watson hasn't brought me, I've brought her. She helps me on my cases."

"Oh?"

"Yes. Now. You were with Zaro Sadozai the night she was injured with acid, weren't you?"

"Yes, but I didn't do it."

"No. Did you see who did?"

"I didn't see anything at all."

"What did you hear?"

"I heard Zaro scream. I heard Khalil shout to get her. That's all."

"Has anything like this ever happened before?"

"To me?"

"Yes. To you. Has anything like this ever happened to you before now?"

"No."

"What about to Ms. Sadozai?"

"Do you mean Zaro?"

"Yes."

"She's been stalking her. I know that."

"Who has been stalking her, Oceane?"

They went on backing and forthing like that for quite awhile. Oceane told Shirley that Zaro's former girlfriend Bori had been stalking Zaro ever since she and Zaro had met, and even before. When she asked why, Zaro said that Bori was a girl who just couldn't let go. She had fallen too hard, and couldn't accept that she didn't feel the same way.

"How many times has Ms. Sadozai been engaged before you, Oceane?"

"We aren't officially engaged."

"How many times has Ms. Sadozai been engaged altogether?"

"Twice."

"So you know about Dody Pearce, the one she was accused of killing?"

"It was an accident. She didn't kill her."

"What do you think happened, Oceane?"

"I know what happened. Zaro told me all about it. They had too much to drink, they were making love, things got a little rough and Dody died."

"Died how?"

"Choked."

"Zaro choked her."

"Not on purpose."

"With her hands?"

"No."

"The autopsy report said the young woman's neck was broken."

"I know."

"And there were bruises like thumbprints on her throat."

"They weren't."

"You weren't there."

"No! But Zaro was. Dody choked to death while they were making love. When Zaro realized what happened, she tried to revive her. She shook her and ... She tried to clear her throat, her mouth, like you're supposed to do, to give her mouth-to-mouth..."

"Or they were fighting and Zaro snapped her neck. The way she was trained to do during the Afghan war. When she was living and fighting as a man."

"That is not what happened. You're trying to turn me against her."

"Has she ever hit you?"

"Of course not! She loves me."

"Has she asked you to marry her?"

"We were planning to get engaged when I turn twenty-one."

"Oceane, you need to see this attempted murder as a wake-up call. Get out now before the next attempt kills you both."

"Don't be ridiculous. No one is going to kill me."

"What if the perpetrator had blown up the boat instead of throwing acid?"

"She didn't. It was Bori, she's not going to kill me. She doesn't even want to kill Zaro. She wanted to hurt her."

"You know how she feels?"

"I'm going back. Zaro is going to be awake and wondering where I am. She needs me to help her."

"She is a wealthy woman, she can hire all the help she needs. She also has a bodyguard. You have to look after yourself, Oceane."

"No! I'm never leaving Zaro, especially not now. She needs me. You don't understand her. She's a loving, caring woman. No one has ever loved me the way Zaro does. We will be together forever. We were going to be together anyway, and now she needs me as much as I need her. If you want to do something useful, go arrest Bori! She's the one who did this." Oceane stood and stormed to the door, which she held open, waiting for us to quickly gather our things and get out. And she made sure the door was locked before she returned the key to the nurses' station.

"Shouldn't I check in on Zaro?" I thought that might give us a reason to extend our time with Oceane.

"Not unless you have results to give her." The ever practical Shirley. I didn't have anything yet, it was too soon. We got into the elevator and headed out for our next stop, and I missed my opportunity to talk with Oceane about the pellets. I was no longer convinced it was a good idea anyway. The pellets certainly wouldn't harm her, they would help her focus on herself, to turn her thoughts inward. But I would have been helping her to do this under false pretenses, and that didn't seem ethical. It seemed too old school, like the days when doctors didn't tell their patients they were dying of cancer, but let them think they had "stomach problems." Or told the patient's spouse instead of the patient. It felt dishonest. I was glad the opportunity had passed.

OCEANE STOPPED JUST OUTSIDE ZARO'S DOOR AND LEANED against the wall as she checked her phone for text messages and voicemail. Inside, Zaro was deep into a phone conversation with her father.

"... cancelled all performances for the next three weeks ... it won't hurt her ratings, her fans know it's because of what happened ... But, Papa, I'm not sure ... well, yes of course, but I can hire people to ... I don't think I want all these paparazzi ... she's no Grace Kelley, she's said nothing about giving it all up to ... anyway, after Dody, and now Bori, I don't think I'll ever marry ... sure ... I love you too. Ciao."

Oceane opened the door, sliding her phone into her pocket.

"Did you miss me? I'm sorry I had to pop out for a few minutes."

Zaro stretched out her arms to embrace Oceane, who ran across the room with tears in her eyes.

Chapter Six:
CONVERSING

OCEANE OPENED THE DOOR TO THE HALLWAY JUST AS Khalil was about to knock.

"Oh! You startled me." She was also aware of his overpowering cologne. He smelled of sandalwood and oranges.

"Pardon me. I came to visit my cousin." He was practically pushing her back inside the room.

"Zaro is resting. I was just stepping out to have a cup of tea. Will you join me?"

"No, thank you. I have to speak with my cousin. We need to discuss some private matters. She will not object to my waking her, I assure you."

"I'll let her know you're here." They were foot to foot in the doorway.

"That's not necessary. Please, go enjoy your tea. We won't be more than half an hour. I'll ring your mobile when we've completed our business. You do have your telephone?" Oceane finally stepped out of Khalil's way and let him pass into the room.

"Yes, of course."

"Very well, Mademoiselle Charles."

Oceane turned her back to Khalil Sadozai and fairly stomped off to the elevator. She knew he had a right to be here, he was family as well as Zaro's employee. She wished she and Zaro were already legally married, as they planned to be. She hoped they would travel to Canada and marry there, never mind that she wasn't twenty-one yet. She decided she would check into the requirements for Canadian same-sex marriage while she had her tea. She could use her Smartphone to look it up. Never mind what Zaro had said to her father. Oceane knew Zaro would marry her. Zaro's relationship with her father was strained and she had probably been lying to him to make him happy.

MEANWHILE KHALIL AND ZARO WENT OVER THE MAIL, THE cables, e-mail, texts, voicemail, and messages that needed Zaro's attention. Zaro had an accountant, an attorney, her Swiss bank accounts manager, an investments account representative, and many others with whom she dealt on a regular basis. She was accustomed to dealing with all these people herself, regularly. Khalil took messages, arranged appointments, organized her calendar, but Zaro made her own decisions. She had no contingency plan to cover an event such as the one she was dealing with now.

"Ibn Al Khala, I have to depend on you now, I'm not able to go to meetings with these people. I can't see, my face is … well, I can't let them see me in this condition. I can't be seen until after I have surgery. I need you to learn my business, enough to fill in for now at least…"

"But Ibn Al Khala, I'm your valet only, I am not a businessman. Surely you want someone more capable to do this…"

"No! I want you. I want my own blood."

"I will do my best."

"That is all I ask."

OCEANE WALKED INTO THE ROOM CARRYING TWO LARGE MUGS on a tray. "Mr. Sadozai, you're still here. I thought you'd be gone by now. Hello, darling. I've brought lattes for us to enjoy. I hope you had a nice visit with your valet."

"I'll be leaving now. I'll come again tomorrow, Ibn Al Khala."

"Tomorrow."

Scarcely had Khalil driven away from the garage than Oceane's cell phone vibrated. "Now who can that be? Sorry, darling. I'll just see who this is."

"Oceane, I heard you were still in Portland, is that true?"

"Of course. I'm with Zaro."

"In the VIP suite?"

"How did you know that?"

"Where else would she be? Listen, would you get me in? I need to see you in the worst way."

"Elijah, I need to take a break from my tour. Can we reschedule for after Zaro recovers?"

"No. Sorry. This is urgent. Can you get me in?"

"When?"

"Like now?"

"Now?"

"I'm downstairs in the lobby."

"You're in the lobby? You start by asking me if I'm in Portland, and you're already in the lobby?"

"Just get me in."

"Fine. I'll wait for you in the hall by the elevator."

She ended the call, made her apology to Zaro, went to the nurses' station and had Elijah admitted to the VIP floor, and waited for him by the elevator as promised. When he appeared, she hardly recognized him. He was still a good half-head taller than she was, but he had lost so much weight he looked like a long distance runner instead of the roly poly guy she was accustomed to seeing. He had also shaved his beard, and let his thin brown hair grow long. All that put together made his blue eyes blaze and his white American teeth gleam. She had to work to keep her own teeth white enough for the publicity people. Maybe he did as well.

"Oceane, it's so good to see you." He pulled her into his arms for a bear hug. She kissed him on both cheeks before asking him what was so important that he was taking her away from her love. After the barest of apologies, he got right to business in the American way.

"I know this is a tragedy for Zaro, sweetheart, but you can't let it derail your career. You are heating up the charts over here right now, and it takes nothing—you hear me, nothing—to send a person tumbling right back down. Especially when they haven't been to the top yet."

"I don't care about that."

"I know you think you don't care about that right now, but you will. In fact, if you love this girl, and I know you do, why you're gonna want to take care of her, am I right?"

"Yes, but. . . ."

"Well, you can't take care of her if you're sitting on the bottom of the charts, honey. You have to get back to work, like right now, and keep going. You are so close. So close I can smell it for you, and you make it, you're gonna be able to support her clear into her old age. Isn't that what you wanna do?"

"She's wealthy beyond my wildest imagination. . ."

"But for how long? I mean, she's injured. Blind, is what I heard. And disfigured? So, who knows? She might not be able to continue to earn, and from what I hear, she's a self-made girl. No money from the parents. I mean what I hear is she's kind of disowned by her family. All on her own. She might have to depend on you in the future. So you'd better have a future, you know what I mean?"

"Do you really think so?"

"I do."

"And of course, I want to be able to provide for her. But I also don't want to leave her when she is so hurt. She needs me. I need to be with her. I don't want to leave her like this."

"She has her valet, right?"

"Well, yes."

"And she can hire people to take care of her. She's in the hospital right now. She can stay as long as she needs to or move to a convalescent hospital."

"I suppose so."

"Maybe your parents would help take care of her?"

"I'm not sure..."

"It's something to look into."

"Elijah, I didn't realize you were so thoughtful."

"Hey, I'm your US Agent. Hell, I'm your international agent, right? Right. I'm the one who books you everywhere outside of France. I have to think about everything that concerns your career outside of your home country. I'm looking out for you and all that concerns you. Everything that affects you affects me, so naturally..."

"I see."

"You're important to me, Oceane. As a person, I mean. Not just because I work for you. I care about you, about what happens to you."

"You hardly know me."

"We met last year in France! We've talked I don't know how many times. Skyped. Texted. Right?"

"Yes, but..."

"Oh, I get it. You Europeans are not as quick to come around as we are. Not as, um..."

"Forward?"

"I guess you could say that. Hell, you just did! That's one of the things I like about you, Oceane, you don't hold back."

"Maybe I too am forward, a little bit."

"We are simpatico."

"Okay."

"Okay! You'll do the concert here? No more nonsense about canceling for the next three weeks? And you'll continue on with your tour?"

"Fine, yes, but when I go to Canada, I want Zaro to join me so we can marry. And she can return to wherever she needs to be for her recovery."

They wrapped up their meeting, which had started in the hallway, meandered to the windows, and ended up back at the elevator.

Oceane again kissed Elijah Reilly's red Irish cheeks and sent him on his way.

When she returned to Zaro they were both more relaxed. Zaro felt better knowing she had taken care of business matters with the help of her cousin. Oceane was bubbling over with excitement for the future, knowing she would be able to care for Zaro as long as she needed her.

That night for the first time since Zaro was attacked, Oceane returned to the yacht to sleep. She was exhausted, and crept aboard hoping not to awaken Khalil. She went straight to the guest cabin, stripped out of her clothes, showered and went to sleep.

WHEN THE DAY SHIFT NURSE DID HIS ROUNDS AT FOUR A.M., he entered Zaro's suite first. All lights were out. The nurse brought up the overhead to full, knowing the patient was blind and would not be bothered. He walked quietly across the room, noting the patient was completely still. As were the tubes and machines. He hurried to the bedside, flung back the covers, and pulled Zaro's head up and back, checking her mouth for obstruction, her throat for a pulse. It was far too late. Her body was already cold. The machine that should have sent out an alarm when the heart stopped was silent. The plug was removed from the wall and the back up battery has been removed from the machine.

The nurse went to the station and called 911.

CHAPTER SEVEN:
HOW DID THIS HAPPEN?

ABOUT A QUARTER AFTER NINE IN THE MORNING SHIRLEY rang and asked me to meet her at the Justice Center. When I asked why, I found myself looking at a screen that showed her icon and a rectangle of options followed by an End bar. She'd already hung up. I had already walked, showered, fed myself and dressed, so I grabbed keys, phone, bag, water and sunglasses and headed for my Smart Car convertible. I didn't get to put the top down as much as I liked in the Pacific NW, but this was a day I could. I put on my baseball cap, snugged it tight, and off I went to downtown Port-land. Parking was a snap with my new car, so I strolled into the Justice Center feeling smug. There I found Shirley waiting, briefcase in hand, eyes steely. My digital watch read 9:38. I thought I'd made great time. Apparently we differed. At least she didn't say so out loud. She went straight to the window for our visitor passes. We were to see Oceane Charles immediately.

Oceane was dressed in a plain white shirt and navy blue cotton pants. Jail wear. I shouldn't have been surprised, we were at the jail, but it was shocking to see a worldwide star in this gear, her face nearly gray with fear, her makeup long gone, her hair limp. Her voice was so quiet I could barely hear her over the shouts of other inmates to their families and lawyers in the visiting room.

"Thank you for coming, Ms. Combs."

"Tell me what happened."

"I don't know what happened, they won't tell me."

"Tell me what happened to you. To yourself."

"Oh. I was asleep. On the boat. I shouldn't have left her. I left her for the first time. I was so tired..." Oceane started to sob.

"Yes, you were tired. So you returned to the yacht for the night, is that it?"

"...I needed to sleep in a bed. I wanted a few hours..."

"And what happened?"

"I went straight to the guest cabin and went to bed. Went to sleep. And early in the morning they were pounding on my door..."

"Who was pounding?"

"The police. They said Zaro was dead and I was a suspect. You have to believe me! I didn't kill her! I loved her!"

"How do they think you killed her?"

"I don't know. They only said she was dead and I must have done it."

"Did you kill her?"

"I told you I didn't kill her! I don't even know how she died. Or what happened. How could this happen? She was on the VIP floor at OHSU, she had security. Who could have hurt her unless it was someone at OHSU? And why would they do that?"

"Those are questions that must be answered."

"Ms. Combs, will you find out for me? Will you help me?"

"Yes, of course, Mademoiselle Charles. I will need you to sign some paperwork."

They completed the contract, I witnessed and notarized it. That's right, I was an official notary for the State of Oregon. Shirley thought of everything. She carried my seal in her briefcase.

As we were leaving the Justice Center, we saw two of Lt. Xio's detectives entering the side door with Austin Beaudet, his hands cuffed behind him. Oceane hadn't mentioned her father being in Portland. The last we'd heard of him was when we said goodnight back in the Loire Valley. Had he come to Portland to attend Oceane's concert—scheduled for tomorrow night and which would surely be cancelled—or had he come for a more sinister purpose?

I went to the office, and Shirley turned around and went back inside the Justice Center to Xio's office. My job was to contact Therese Beaudet and see what she knew. Shirley was going to find out everything she could about the murder and the list of suspects.

Mine was the far simpler task. Therese had heard nothing at all. So although my job was simple, it wasn't easy. I was in the awkward position of informing her that both her beloved daughter and her husband were now residents of the Justice Center, suspected of murdering the very woman we were hired to keep her daughter away from. I assured her that Oceane appeared well, and was being looked after, that she had signed a contract with Shirley only minutes before. I told her that Shirley was with Austin at that moment (possible small fib as I didn't really know what Shirley was doing at that second), and we would contact her again as soon as we knew when both Austin and Oceane were being granted bail. I took it a step further and arranged with her for bail to be made available, as this could be a lengthy process when dealing internationally. I used Shirley's financial investment firm to set up the account, transfer in funds from the Beaudet's bank, and we were ready to make bail for either or both parties when they were arraigned. Presumably the next day.

I left all the pertinent information with Lix, and went out on my two scheduled house calls. I kept my cell on in case Shirley called, but the afternoon went by without interruption.

I was crossing the Hawthorne Bridge on my return to the office when Shirley's ringtone sounded. I didn't answer, of course. It's against the law to speak or text on your cell phone in Oregon. Unless you are parked. As the Beatles cried out their fourth "Help!" I simultaneously slammed on my brakes and slid the unlock bar on my iPhone. The bridge was up. I put the car in park, turned the engine off as Shirley told me to get to the office right away so she could fill me in in person. I told her I was merely blocks away, but with the bridge up, I'd probably be at least fifteen minutes, did she want to relate anything while we waited? No, but I could pick up a couple of coffees on my way up.

All those cars, headed both West (me) and East (commuters) were held up for one measly, yes measly, sailboat whose captain was inconsiderate enough to be out sightseeing on the Willamette in the middle of the city at rush hour. Were there no rules about this? I guessed if the sails were high enough to cause the bridge to be lifted, the owners had enough clout to sail around whenever they liked. Especially during Rose Festival time. I took several deep breaths. I wouldn't even care, or probably even notice, if Shirley weren't waiting on the other side of the bridge with her hard eyes. I was such a people pleaser. It was one thing to be nurturing, a good trait to have as a doctor of natural medicine. It was another to be so concerned about pleasing others that I caused myself stress. More breathing was needed. The truth was Shirley had other things on her mind than how many minutes she had to wait for me. She was at that moment busy on the case, or something else. My not being there at her beck and call was a fleeting irritation. One more breath. There, I felt better. The bridge was back down. I zoomed across, parked the car in a space too small for a compact car, but not for me, picked up two coffees and headed up to the office.

"Mary, where have you been all afternoon? I need you on this case!" Shirley actually raised her voice. I felt my face flush as Lix looked up at us, her eyebrows raised.

"What's up, Shirl? Here, take your coffee, and let's go into your office."

That shut her up. I saw a slight tinge of pink crawl up her neck as she turned to walk into her office. I smiled at Lix and she gave me a thumbs up at desk level as I followed behind.

Shirley and I settled right into the business at hand, which was everything she had learned from Lt. Xio. The coffee was hot, and the aroma coupled with that small encouragement from Lix was enough to boost my confidence. But Shirley's words were welcome too.

"Thanks for coming back after your home visits this afternoon, Mary. I really needed you on this case."

"How so?" I mean, I knew she wanted me to take notes at the interviews, but she could always use a recorder if I couldn't make it. I often felt I was along more for my own curiosity than because Shirley needed a sidekick.

"Your people skills, of course. I didn't develop socially as I grew up. You did. You must have noticed by now how often I rely on your skills in this area during interviews?"

"I wouldn't say rely."

"What would you say?"

"Include. You include me."

"You give me credit for social skills I don't have. It doesn't occur to me to 'include' you. When I notice the interview faltering due to a lack on my part, I shift it to you to take over for me."

"Oh."

"Indeed. Oh. Mary, I am frustrated by your lack of observation, even in such a benign instance as this."

"That isn't fair!"

"Why not?"

"Because it is benign. I'm trying to be more observant in our cases when things are really important. I didn't know I was supposed to be so observant of personal instances of our own behavior as well."

"Everything is important. No, more than that. Everything is critical. You have to learn to observe everything as if your life depends on it, Mary because it might."

"That makes me tired."

"Maybe you aren't cut out for this work."

"Maybe I'm not."

"I hope that's not so. Especially right now because we are in the middle of an important case."

"I won't walk out on you, if that's what you're worried about."

"Not literally and not figuratively either?"

"No. Can we get back to your telling me what happened today?"

"Of course."

She did. That's one thing you can always count on with Shirley. She can turn on a dime. She won't harangue you about an "issue" all evening if you don't want to talk about it. Of course she might not talk to you about your burning issue at all if she's tied up with a problem she's trying to solve, even if her problem doesn't seem important to you. I couldn't stand being around people who wouldn't let something drop when I needed to take a break though, so this was a good working relationship for me. I was going to have to up my observational game. She made it seem so easy. Believe me, it was not. For example, while I was thinking about how great it was that Shirley could let something go, she was telling me about something that happened at the PPB while Lt. Xio was briefing her. I missed the entire thing. Not only that, but she got up, walked around the desk and got something out of the cabinet, did something with it and put it back, but I failed to note what it was. Now I would have to ask her about all that, or hope it wasn't important (or critical!) to anything we had going on.

CHAPTER EIGHT:
XIO TIMES IT RIGHT

I WAS PAYING ATTENTION NOW. HERE'S WHAT I LEARNED: Lt. Xio gave Shirley the complete rundown. He knew Shirley's methods and he also knew she would give her full attention to solving Zaro Sadozai's murder. While the case was high profile and would command attention from his own team, he would have to spend time keeping the mayor happy, the publicity hounds happy, the investigative reporters out of his thinning hair, and playing diplomat to the international crowd involved in this already growing circus of a case. First, Zaro Sadozai was a wealthy woman with a lurid past the media were busy making meals of in the hours since her death. Second, her fiancée Oceane Charles was an international pop star about to make her US debut here in Portland, and a suspect in the suspicious death. Third, Zaro's former girlfriend, Borbála (Bori) Eszti, the prime suspect, was out on bail for having attempted to murder her already, and Bori was a look alike for Uma Thurman. Naturally, the paparazzi were stalking her every move.

By relying on Shirley to investigate and share what she learned with him, Lt. Xio saved himself valuable time and person power, and more important (to him), he saved the government money. If money were no object and he could hire all the people he needed to do the job, he would neither need nor use Shirley Combs. He knew it. She knew it. We all ignored it because money is an object, so why bother our heads?

Xio also knew that despite Shirley's undisputed lack of social niceties, she would do him little harm in the diplomacy area because she had me. I now realized this was an area where I was particularly useful in this partnership. I handled many aspects of our business, especially the areas where I had skills superior to Shirley's. There weren't that many areas, so I looked alive when they turned up. I would do better in all of them from now on. Our talk woke me up.

So far, Xio's team had identified four suspects: Bori, of course; Oceane, unfortunately; Austin—why did he show up when he did? And Zaro's valet/cousin, Khalil. According to the Portland Police Bureau, each of these people had no alibi, and could have gotten into Zaro's VIP room at OHSU and killed her.

As for how she died, according to the medical examiner, Zaro was given an overdose of morphine, probably in her IV line while she was sleeping. Further tests would be run, of course, but the full toxicology reports wouldn't be back for a week or more. The autopsy was completed within hours after her death, due to her VIP status.

Xio's team members were interviewing the suspects that day. All four were expected to be arraigned the next morning and to be allowed to make bail, although the bail amounts would be set at amounts commensurate with their status.

"I think it best that we hie ourselves over to the Justice Center and begin interviewing the suspects right behind the team," said Shirley.

"I think we ought to have dinner first. Keep our strength up. We don't know how long we might have to be over there." I won and we ate our pad Thai standing up at the food truck.

"We'll interview Bori first. And Austin, and finally Khalil. We'll stop in and speak with Oceane, to fill her in on what we've learned." It seemed Shirley always made the plans.

"How about a couple of stops before we headed to the jail. First, Voodoo Doughnuts for the cops on duty, and second to Rite-Aid for some grooming aids for each of the suspects and Oceane?" I knew they got a bar of soap and a comb, but please.

"Good idea, Mary."

At Voodoo we bought three dozen: a box of mixed doughnuts, a box of voodoo dolls, and a box of bacon maple bars. At Rite-Aid, we bought gift sets for everyone. The sets contained lotion, body wash, a scrubby, and deodorant, plus additional organic shampoo, conditioner, and toothpaste. We also bought each person packets of individual tooth-cleaners in case they weren't being allowed toothbrushes (those can be sharpened into weapons). I had my extra foldie totes, so we used those to pack up everything. Otherwise we'd have been loaded down with the mandatory paper bags shops had provide now that plastic was forbidden.

We were welcomed with smiles when the pink Voodoo boxes appeared. Cops and doughnuts may be a stereotype, but Voodoo Doughnuts are always a big hit. I didn't eat them myself, but the sight of that box, the smell of all that sugar, and the smiles on other people's faces never failed to cheer me up. Of course, as a naturopath, I didn't advocate eating doughnuts on a regular basis. Or bringing them to potlucks or anything like that. Use them sparingly, that was my advice.

Bori was almost happy to see us. Maybe she was only glad to see the gift basket and toiletries, but at least she looked relieved, and her body language was more open than the last time we spoke with her. She kept her arm curled around the goodies, as if we might snatch them back, but leaned back in the chair and kept her head up, her face relaxed as she greeted us.

"Why are you here? Did my attorney send you?"

"I'm representing another client, Bori, so I can't help you in that sense. However, I am here to uncover the truth, to investigate the matter of Ms. Sadozai's death. That may help you, if you're willing to talk with us."

"Okay. I might need your help. My attorney was provided by the government. I'm scared. The police think I killed her."

"I see. What evidence do they have that leads them to think that?"

"They don't have evidence. They just don't believe me when I say I didn't do it."

"Where were you when Ms. Sadozai died?"

"If she died during last night, I was in my room asleep."

"Alone?"

"Of course alone."

"People are not always alone, so there is no of course. Can anyone vouch for your being alone in your room all night?"

"I don't think so. I don't have an armed guard standing outside my door, or a nanny sitting at my bedside. I had to move to a hotel though. Couch surfing people weren't happy when they heard I was accused of attempted murder. Kicked me out of their condo, and they moved out of my home. As if they might catch something by being in my house."

"Which hotel are you staying in, and your room number please?"

I noted she was at the Benson, room 515. Like most hotels, they used electronic keys, and we could trace the times she unlocked her door. No doubt the police had already done so. I would check with them before I called the Benson.

We left Bori carrying her gifts to her cell, no doubt headed to the showers at the first opportunity. Next up was Austin Beaudet. I dreaded seeing him here, but Shirley went forward with the same stride she used when we greeted him at his villa in France.

"Monsieur Beaudet." She stuck out her right hand. He motioned her toward him and kissed each of her cheeks. She was a bit non-plussed, but recovered as he gestured for me to come to him. He was handcuffed to the table, of course.

"Doctor Watson, how lovely to see you, even in this dreadful cir-cumstance." I received and returned the kisses, noticing he already smelled of the jail soap as opposed to how he'd smelled when I met him in France. And I crossed to Shirley's side to take notes as the two of them sat across from each other.

"Ms. Combs, I hope you are here to release me from this horrible place. I never thought to spend time in your city's prison."

"What did you expect to do here in Portland, M. Beaudet?"

"I came to watch Oceane perform ... and I confess, I hoped to convince her to leave that woman and return to France afterwards."

"Did Oceane know you were coming?"

"*Non*. It was a surprise. I meant to telephone her this morning and invite her to lunch with me, but before this could happen, the police came and arrested me. For nothing! I was simply having *le café* at le Starbucks!"

"They arrested you at Starbucks?"

"*Oui*. Right down the street from my hotel. I've never been so embarrassed."

"How did they know where to find you?"

"The hotel doorman told them where I had gone. I asked him where to get *le café* at six a.m., and he gave me directions. They found me *tres vite*."

"So they know where you were from that point on."

"Yes, and they know I arrived at the hotel at midnight. After that I have no one to tell where I was."

"No confirmed alibi."

"They suspect you in Ms. Sadozai's death."

"It is ridiculous. I would not kill anyone."

"Not even to protect your daughter?"

"Oceane was not in danger!"

"I believe you hired me to rescue her from this 'scoundrel' this 'dangerous person' isn't that what you said, M. Beaudet?"

"But Madame, surely you can't believe I would kill the woman myself!"

"I see."

"*Non*! I did not kill her, I did not have her killed. I had nothing to do with the death of this terrible woman."

"Your daughter has hired me to help clear her name."

"What? I do not understand your meaning."

"Your daughter Oceane. She is also a suspect in this case."

"This is an outrage! That is even more unbelievable. What is wrong with the Americans? You can believe that a young woman like Oceane would attack and kill another woman? Even a person such as Zaro Sadozai? It makes more logic to believe that her father, that I would do such a thing, even though I did not. Oh, I must telephone Therese. Does Therese know this?"

I took that one. "I spoke with Madame Beaudet earlier. I let her know that both of you are in custody, that we would be speaking with both of you this evening, and you are in good hands with us. She is fine, Monsieur, but she cannot leave the vineyards to come here as there is no one to take over the management at this time. She said you would understand."

"But of course. Thank you for speaking with her. That is so kind. I should have asked about Oceane. I am so selfish. I had no idea they would have arrested her as well. That is police brutality. You must do something. You must get her out of here. Money is not a problem, we have enough."

"Both of you will be arraigned in court tomorrow morning, I'm sure. Have you seen your attorney yet?"

"*Non.* No attorney. They said one would be appointed for me, as I know no one here."

"We'll call someone for you. Do you want this on your own account, or on Oceane's?"

"On my own, of course."

"Very well. We will continue to consult with you only on the matter of getting you released. We'll send you a final bill for our services, as Oceane is no longer with Zaro Sadozai. From here on we are involved as representatives of Oceane only, and will consult directly with her unless she asks us to speak with you. Understood?"

"Yes, I understand. But you will tell me which attorney is the one you send, or how will I know?"

"The attorney we send will let you know. Any attorney sent by the state will have to say so, and in any case, should not show up once we inform the police that we have engaged an attorney on your behalf."

All questions asked and answered, we moved on, stopping only for a glass of water and for me to check my notes and get out fresh paper.

Khalil was soon attached to the table by handcuffs, just as all prisoners were before we were allowed to question them. He had on the same uniform as the rest. He managed to make it look fresh and stylish. Maybe it was his shiny black hair, gorgeous olive skin, or sparkling black eyes, but he looked like a movie star. The tee shirt was as blindingly white as his teeth when he smiled as he stood to greet us. His scent was that of a male model in a magazine. How did he do that? He must wear expensive toilet water, and he must not have washed it off. I felt almost irresistibly drawn to him. That smell made me miss my father. What was it? Musk? Vanilla? I couldn't quite place it.

"Ladies, what a welcome change. What brings you here?"

"We've come to question you in the death of your employer Zaro Sadozai, Mr. Sadozai."

His face changed immediately to one of appropriate sadness. "Ah, yes, such a tragedy. First, my dear cousin was attacked by Bori with the acid, and she came back and killed her. It is a common occurrence among people who are so obsessed, I think."

"You have no doubt that the killer was Bori?"

"None. Bori has been stalking Zaro for so long. Many months. Finally she was able to attack Zaro with the acid and blind her, burn her so severely Zaro was in hospital. Bori must have done it. Who else would do such a thing?"

"The police seem to have several suspects. Including you."

"They are being overly vigilant, I think."

"How so?"

"Americans. They overdo everything, isn't it? Everything bigger, more of it. Too many troops in Afghanistan, too many bombs, too many cars, too much food, everyone too fat. So. Too many suspects. Is logical. I didn't kill my cousin. They will not keep me here for long."

"Where were you last night from midnight to four a.m.?"

"I was in bed asleep."

"Alone?"

"Of course I was alone. I was working. I was onboard the ship."

"Can anyone vouch for you?"

"What do you mean?"

"Can someone confirm that?"

"No. The crew had the night off. They were out past midnight. I don't know what time they came in because I was sleeping. I didn't get up, so they didn't see me and I didn't see them."

"What about Oceane?"

"What about her?"

"Did you see her?"

"No. She has been spending all her time at the hospital."

"What time did you say you went to bed last night?"

"Ten o'clock. The crew was out, I had nothing more to do, and I had a long day. I went to bed early and read for awhile. I fell asleep and woke up when the police pounded on my door about six a.m."

"What book were you reading?"

"The Diwan of Rahman Baba."

"Does your copy contain all 343 poems?"

"Yes, as a matter of fact, it does. You are familiar?"

"Only in English. You read it in Pashto?"

"My copy is in Pashto, and most of the poems are written in that language. But I can read it in English as well."

"We will talk again soon."

I couldn't miss the opportunity, I had to know. "Excuse me, but what is that scent you're wearing?"

"I don't understand."

"Cologne? After shave?"

"It's only an essential oil. Zaro gave it to me. Egyptian musk, I think."

"Thank you." Musk, of course. My dad used to wear a light musk oil. Funny how scent is such a trigger of memories for us. More than visual or sound, they say.

With that we left Khalil Sadozai and prepared for our visit with Oceane. We wanted to be sure we gave her a concise rundown of everything we knew regarding the suspects, her family, and the death of her fiancée. A call had come in from Attorney Hala Cumfer. She would represent both Austin and Oceane Beaudet at their arraignments. After that, she would choose one or the other to defend, and another attorney would need to be brought in for the other. It was critical that both had the best possible defense and there be no conflict of interest.

When we went to the desk to ask for Oceane, we were told we wouldn't be allowed to see her that night. Lt. Xio wouldn't take Shirley's calls, my friend on the switchboard told me only that a doctor had been called, and he thought it might have been for "the French girl." Nobody else would tell us anything more than thanks for the doughnuts. We were in for a sleepless night.

CHAPTER NINE:
IT WAS NOTHING

LIX CALLED THE JUSTICE CENTER LINES REPEATEDLY BEGIN-
ning at fifteen seconds before the hour until the first operator
picked up. Once we knew that Oceane was not in the hospital, was
at the Justice Center and available for visiting, Shirley and I picked
up another three boxes of Voodoo doughnuts and headed straight
there. We didn't hang around to collect our thanks, we were interested only in our client.

She looked a bit like Kristen Stewart in *Twilight* at her palest.
Pasty complexion, even thinner than yesterday if that were possible,
her eyes dull. Her hair was shiny though. She had obviously tried out
the hair products we brought.

"We heard a doctor was called for you. What happened?" That
was Shirley. All business, as usual.

"I fainted. It was nothing."

"Nothing? What did they say was the cause?"

"I hadn't eaten, and my blood pressure was low. They gave me
orange juice, and had me drink a large quantity of water. I tried to
eat what they gave me, but truly it was inedible."

"Shirley, we have to get her some food in here."

"Not if we get you out of here this morning, Ms. Charles. Have
you spoken with your attorney yet?"

"I saw a Hala Cumfer."

"Yes, that's the one."

"She said I would be arraigned at ten a.m. I don't know what that means, arraigned."

"Arraignment is the court proceeding where you will be formally charged with a crime, plead guilty or not guilty, and bail will be set. I expect Ms. Cumfer will advise you to plead not guilty, bail will be set, and you will pay it and be released."

"What about *mon pere*?"

"The same will be true for your father."

"And Ms. Cumfer will represent us at our trials?"

"You will have to decide which of you chooses to hire Ms. Cumfer, if either of you does, and another attorney from another firm must be hired to represent the other person in your family."

"Why? Why can't she represent both of us? We could all be together, I could be with my father more this way."

"It would be a conflict of interest, Ms. Charles."

I saw that she was confused. "It's a legal term, Oceane. It's just the way it has to be. I'm sure you and your father will find time to be together."

I didn't tell her that they wouldn't be allowed to discuss the case with each other. She was going to learn these hard facts of life soon enough.

After Shirley quickly updated Oceane on what we learned from our meetings with Austin and Khalil the day before, the guard came and took our client away. It was time for her to prepare for the short walk to court. For this she would have to change into the bright orange jump suit. I handed her a brand new tangerine lipstick I picked up that morning at Walgreen's on the way in to work.

"Here. Put this on. You'll feel better."

She gave us a wan smile as she turned to leave the room.

ON THE WAY BACK TO THE OFFICE SHIRLEY SUGGESTED WE GET on the Max light-rail instead and make a visit to Elijah Reilly. The

Max line runs right in front of our office building, so we walked to the stop that would get us on the Blue Line headed to Gresham, bought our tickets and validated them as soon as we saw the train coming. As usual the train was full of people and bikes. Tourists, skateboarders, elders, mothers, babies, young people, shoppers headed for Lloyd Center, workers, and a few homeless riding the train in fareless square. The homeless would get off at Lloyd Center and catch the train returning downtown and make the loop over and over to fill some time.

There were not so many homeless out on sunny days like today. What would I do if I faced that life? No doubt I would do as so many people do. We always hear that people are a paycheck away from living on the streets, and while that isn't the case for me, I know that I am privileged. I'm not under the illusion that I somehow earned the right to the roof I have, the education, my car, my good health, all because I was smart enough, or slim enough, or something. I was lucky to be born to parents in the middle class. They were also white, Protestant, had good work ethics, and were educated. They saved for my and my sister Tommy's education. Tommy didn't live to collect, so I was able to use her funds to go on to naturopathic college. Because I didn't have student loans I was able to save up to buy a house someday. As I didn't have children or debt, I was able to afford a new car. I didn't do anything to excess: drink, eat, or spend. I didn't smoke, do drugs or gamble. I wore simple, well-made clothing, and I had only one pet. So I was able to save and to support the charities whose values I shared. I considered myself fortunate.

Soon enough we were de-boarding the train. We weren't in Gresham, but we were fairly close to the line that divides Portland and Gresham. We were at 162nd and E. Burnside. Burnside divided north from south Portland. The Willamette River divided east from west. That makes up the four quadrants. Some people called North Portland the "fifth quadrant" because its streets don't fit neatly into the NE, SE, NW, SW with the others.

Where we were, there were apartment complexes, most of them twenty years old or so. Rents out there were lower than closer to downtown, and the apartments had more square footage, if poorer views. Crime was sometimes a problem around the Max line out there as well, although Tri Met had added extra transit police at night. Shirley walked straight up to the address as if she had been here before and rang the bell. I looked around, noticing cats in the parking lot, and a barking dog in a nearby apartment. I heard quick footsteps before the door was yanked open.

"I don't want any Jehovah's Witness crap."

"Mr. Reilly, I'm Shirley Combs. This is Dr. Mary Watson. We represent Oceane Charles."

"What? Who?"

"Shirley Combs. Watson."

"What about Oceane?"

"We represent her."

"How? I mean I represent her. Internationally. So if you think you're gonna horn in on that somehow…"

"My card."

He studied Shirley's card for at least a minute, even looking at the back. I've seen her do that many times, but I can't imagine that he would have actually observed anything. He was buying time.

"May we come in?"

"Oh right. Right. Sure, okay, but my place is. Well, my house-keeper hasn't been here…"

"It's fine."

He stood back and let us inside. His housekeeper had never been there.

He kicked a path for us as we made our way through the hall that contained the washer and dryer into the living room. There was a couch and chair, a large screen television and approximately 6,000 pizza boxes, an equal amount of beer cans, potato chip bags, shoes, sweats, tee shirts, hoodies, a comforter, some pillows, an array of electronics scattered in and around, and a gallon of milk that looked a bit thick. Elijah bent in half, kicking and scooping, creating places for us to sit down. Shirley and I sat on the edge of the couch while he piled into the chair. As he did, the comforter edges puffed up around him and loud sounds of crunching came from beneath him. Potato chips was my guess.

"You hungry? Can I get you anything?"

"No, that's okay, we're fine." I spoke for both of us. I didn't want to hear what Shirley might say in this situation.

"Mr. Reilly, are you aware that Ms. Charles has been accused of murder?"

"No."

"I see. Thank you for your time, Mr. Reilly. We can see ourselves out."

We stood to leave.

"What? Wait. You're going now?"

"Yes. Thank you for your hospitality."

We left Elijah Reilly standing in his living room with his mouth hanging open.

I kept my own mouth shut as we hurried back to the Max stop. We still had enough time on our tickets to use the same ones we rode out on to get back downtown to our office. Even though public transportation was cheap, I loved to save money. That's frugal. That's common sense. That's a little over two bucks I could put in my rainy day fund. These were my thoughts on the way to the train, while Shirley was no doubt thinking about the case. Once we were on the train, this time with plenty of seats, and space all around us, I decided to get a few answers.

"Why didn't you ask Elijah more questions?"

"I got all the information I needed."

"You didn't even interrogate him!"

"Nevertheless."

"So you know he lives in a messy apartment."

"I knew that already."

"How did you know that already?"

"I called on Mr. Reilly last night."

"And why didn't he recognize you?"

"He wasn't home last night."

"You broke in?"

"No. I could smell the interior from the door. The shades were askew. The doorknob itself was grimy, I thought perhaps you noticed that today? Yes, it was still the same today. Smeared a bit more. The door mat is beyond utility, surely you saw that? From the appearance of the outside, one could hardly expect the inside to be in anything but worse condition."

"Now that you mention it, I did notice the mat."

"Mm."

"You asked if he knew about Oceane being in jail."

"I asked if he knew she has been charged with murder."

"He didn't. But. Oh! He didn't react. He didn't ask us anything. So, you think he did it?"

"It's curious that he says he didn't know she was charged with murder, and he is her international representative, yet he asked us nothing. Not who she might have killed or why, or where she is, or how she is, or what happened, or how he can see her. Just no."

"He must have been thinking what to say next."

"Indeed."

"Maybe he was stunned."

"Did he run after us? Telephone me? He does have my card."

"Right. But do you think he killed Zaro? How would he do it? And why? Is he in love with Oceane? He's hardly her type, I mean even if she were straight. Look at him. He's almost twice her age, balding, and what a slob."

"We follow the clues, Doctor. All of them. Each is suggestive in itself. Together they have a cumulative force."

"Words to live by, if I'm not mistaken."

She chuckled. I knew her methods.

As we rode back to downtown, I kept an ear open for Shirley's cell phone, expecting that Elijah Reilly would telephone her any minute. He didn't. I thought perhaps his thinking was as sloppy as his housekeeping. Maybe he had someone else to call for answers. He would surely call Oceane, or try to. I wondered how he became her international representative and whether she had any idea what a slob he was in his personal life. Was I being biased? I'd seen documentaries of rock stars in which they all lay about in horrible messes. Did that messiness extend to their managers and representatives? I'd seen signs that a messy desk was a sign of an organized mind, or something to that effect. In my way, I had dismissed it because that sentiment didn't fit my personal values. It occurred to me that if I were to be a better detective, I needed to keep an open mind, and simply observe what was true, rather than what met or didn't meet my own set of principles.

Shirley grabbed my attention by stating that we needed to make a trip to the morgue. When I left medical school I thought I had seen all the dead animals and cadavers I'd ever have to see or touch. Of course I might witness the death of a dear patient at some point. Never did I dream that I would become the assistant to a consulting detective and begin to see dead bodies on a regular basis. Not just dead, but murdered. Life has a way of throwing outrageous curves into every journey. Now I was about to have to view the lifeless body of Zado Sadozai, when only days ago I was trying to help her heal.

CHAPTER TEN:
TO THE MORGUE

S HIRLEY DECIDED TO GO ALONE TO THE MORGUE TO VIEW the body. I wasn't disappointed. She wanted to have a personal chat with Medical Examiner Dr. Wentworth who had recently transferred from Lake Oswego to Portland. He may have considered it a step down rather than the promotion it was, knowing how much the Lake Oswegans value their town over the City of Roses. Realistic people usually valued money and size of staff over snob appeal, but not everyone did. Even though Lake Oswego had higher real estate taxes, Portland paid higher salaries for its ME staff. Dr. Wentworth had reached the top of his salary range at Lake Oswego at $91,000. He was able to start in Portland at $150,000. All these facts were available on the internet, free for nosy parkers like me. Or investigators like Shirley. If I hadn't liked my little house so much, I would have left it and moved to Portland. When I moved out to Oregon I had no idea I was moving into a suburb known for being white, cliquish, and scared of Portland. I happened on a good deal on rent, liked being on a lake, not too far from the city, and I was accustomed to having to commute. Maybe I would think about buying my own house somewhere in the city. If I did, I was going to move to a neighborhood I could walk in, close to a MAX line, close to a coffeehouse I liked, maybe some food trucks nearby, but I wanted Martha to be safe too. And I wanted a garden.

DR. EUGENE WENTWORTH LEFT SHIRLEY ALONE IN THE ROOM with Zaro's body, which he pulled from one of the drawers, and placed onto a gurney, with the help of a lift system installed for the purpose. Zaro had been autopsied, so she had the noticeable "Y" scar on her chest and torso. Her brain also had been removed and weighed, along with all her other organs. There was no sign of fear on her face, which was relaxed as though she had never woken. The skin was blackened around her eyes and on her eyelids where the acid had burned her. Her hands were also blackened where she had automatically brought them to her eyes after the acid was shot at her. They had begun to heal, so there were streaks of pink where the burnt flesh had been debrided, some areas of yellow that would have been cleaned away the night before she died.

Shirley looked Zaro over from head to toe and back again, observing every detail. Once the body was returned to the chamber, she sat with Dr. Wentworth in his office while he went over the report. Cause of death: morphine overdose. Zaro had been on a prescribed dose of ten mg morphine every four hours. She had a pump, and could administer the dosage herself, but there were safety procedures in place that made it impossible for her to overdose herself. She could take her morphine half an hour early, or not take it at all, but she could not accidentally overdose via the pump.

Someone had inserted the extra morphine into her IV line. No needle marks were found on her body, and Dr. Wentworth searched carefully, everywhere. Shirley had done so as well.

Shirley needed to visit the crime scene in order to determine how someone was able to administer two hundred mg of morphine to Zaro Sadozai in the middle of the night without being noticed.

WHILE SHIRLEY WAS AT THE MORGUE, I WAS ON THE PHONE with my friends at Portland Police Bureau. First I talked to Inez Lopez who was a rookie in uniform on the bicycle city policing unit.

She was so much fun to go biking with. She knew downtown inside and out, and she would tell me almost anything that went on in the department because she knew I wouldn't reveal my source. And I have been able to help her with some medical issues she didn't want to appear in her City records. She couldn't help me get Shirley into OHSU's VIP floor, but she sent me to Dorothy Pelham in Human Resources. Normally, I stick with the cops who work the cases, but Inez gave me a referral. So I talked to Dorothy. She said HR doesn't like to get involved with outside consultants, but as I was a friend of Inez, she did know the PR person up at OHSU and maybe he would help me. His name was Otis Jefferson. Mr. Jefferson was a nice enough man. Or seemed so on the phone. He was a public information office man really, though so who knew? He did say he would meet me and Ms. Combs at the VIP Hall, and let us into Ms. Sadozai's room as we were her representatives. Would three p.m. be a good time? Yes sir, it would be perfect. I put the time on my and Shirley's calendars on our smartphones, knowing that meant she would get an instant text.

At three p.m. sharp, we met Otis Jefferson at the outer door to the VIP Hall at OHSU. He towered over both of us, and reminded me of an old Trail Blazer basketball player Clyde Drexler, with his shaved head, toothy smile, and deep voice. His tailored suit must have come from a big and tall shop because OHSU does not pay enough for custom-made.

"I've heard of you, Ms. Combs, so the Portland Police called you in on this case, did they?"

"I'm representing Oceane Charles, Mr. Jefferson."

"Oh."

"I need to see the room now."

"You mean representing, like a lawyer? You suing OHSU?"

"I'm here to find out who murdered Zaro Sadozai. I'm not suing anyone."

"That's what I thought. You're like a detective. Right?"

"I am a detective. I am a private investigator, hired by Oceane Charles. Now may we please go to the room where Zaro Sadozai was killed?"

"Sorry."

He buzzed the door, and answered with his credentials when the intercom buzzed back. Once inside we got into the elevator, and he used his key to get us to the appropriate floor. From there we went to the nurses' station and were vetted by the nurse in charge before he led us to Zaro's room, which was sealed with police tape. And he left us alone as Shirley began her examination and I took notes, being careful to follow in her wake, never to get ahead of her, or in her way.

Even though it wasn't a rainy day, I was glad we weren't outdoors for this excursion. It was a relief to be in a controlled environment. No wind, no birds or bugs or animals. No tourists or other citizens. No excrement. And in this case, not even any blood. We pulled on our coveralls, our shoe covers, got out our magnifying glasses, our baggies, labels, and pens, pulled on our tight latex-free gloves and set to work covering every inch of the space. The PPB had already done this of course, so now we were picking up their fibers, or whatever they left behind. I took pictures of every clue, the room from every angle, the furniture including the bed, the window, the door, the locks, and all the equipment, switches, the bathroom and all its fixtures, switches, knobs and pulls.

Zaro died in her sleep in a hospital bed. No signs of struggle. This was the cleanest murder case we had investigated so far. The sheets were barely wrinkled, let alone disturbed. According to the records, Zaro died between midnight and two a.m., so her body was already cool to the touch, and rigor mortis was just beginning when she was discovered at four.

By seven p.m., my stomach was growling and we were wrapping up our examination of the room. I had taken approximately 15 million photos of the ICU monitor that had been unplugged from Zaro Sadozai without alarming the nurses. It was unplugged from the wall.

We still had to learn why the nurse didn't know Zaro was in trouble and died. We needed to confirm she was being monitored during the night of her death.

When we were ready to leave the building, we found Otis Jefferson at the nurses' station ready to escort us out.

"Were you able to get everything you need, detective?"

"We will need to speak with the nurse who found the body, as well as the Chief nurse in charge that night."

"I can arrange those interviews for you. I'll have to check the schedule. May I call you tomorrow?"

"That will have to do."

I stuck out my hand and shook his, trying to make nice for both myself and Shirley, even though I felt tired and grumpy. It would do. Tomorrow would be there soon enough.

Over dinner at Screen Door on East Burnside, where I had a plate of all local organic sides and Shirley had one side salad and fresh cornbread, we went over our list of evidence. It was paltry. I'll admit I was far more interested in my salad of marinated beets with baby red and green romaine lettuces, grapefruit, navel oranges, pistachios, goat cheese & citrus vinaigrette. Still, there wasn't much evidence. All those pictures of the monitoring equipment showed nothing. How the heck did someone manage to unplug the equipment without alerting the nurses? That was the question. The back-up battery had been removed. But when it was still plugged in, it should have alarmed. Or maybe it was dead. How convenient. Didn't those batteries have to be inspected, like smoke alarms? Something for Lix to look into. I made a note.

The timing was also convenient. The nurses changed shifts at midnight. The overdose occurred sometime between midnight and two a.m. and Zaro wasn't looked in on until four a.m. according to her chart. The murderer had entered her room, injected her IV line with a lethal dose of morphine and left, all without being noticed, apparently comfortable in the knowledge that her body wouldn't be discovered until the nurse checked on her at four a.m. Yet, as we all knew, there were security systems in place for her protection, obstacles to keep strangers or people who might harm Zaro from getting to her. Those systems had failed. Buzzers, IDs, check-ins, nothing had worked.

Everything pointed to an accomplice. I said as much to Shirley.

"It would seem so."

"Who do you think it is?"

"Lt. Xio and his team will begin interviewing the hospital staff shortly if they aren't already doing so."

"You talked to him?"

"It's logical."

I knew she wanted to say it was elementary.

The drive back to Lake Oswego seemed longer than it ever had before. Maybe it was the pouring rain on the soft-top of the car. Or the fact I'd have to be at the office in less than twelve hours. Or maybe it was the fact that I'd seen a for sale sign on a sweet bungalow as I drove through the inner SE neighborhood, before crossing the Ross Island Bridge on my way back home. I told my iPhone to remember the name and number of Beth Adams, Real Estate agent.

CHAPTER ELEVEN:
ACCUSED STAR
TO BE ARRAIGNED

B Y MORNING THE SUN WAS OUT AGAIN, I PUT THE CON-
vertible top down on the way to the office and fairly flew into
Portland. Buy a house? Move? Was I crazy? Forget Beth Adams. I
pulled into the smallest parking space ever, put the top up, and
popped into the coffee spot for my morning buzz. *The Oregonian*
had Oceane's picture above the fold. The headline was "Accused Star
to be Arraigned" which was benign enough, but the story ripped her
to shreds. It made it seem like Oceane was the only possible suspect
because they were engaged, she was at the hospital with Zaro, and
had no confirmed alibi. The paper made little mention of the fact
that the other suspects had no alibis, or that they were even suspected. Oceane's name sold papers. I was steamed. Shirley was calm.
She didn't understand why I was upset. The media had a part to play.
They were playing it. We had to do our own job and ignore them
unless we needed them to fulfill our own purpose, which we didn't at
the moment. I was about to suggest we go out for coffee for a change,
when Shirley took a call and went into her office and shut the door.
She also turned her back to me. These two things together told me
this was an unusual call. Personal? Shirley didn't usually keep secrets
per se, so why was she turning her back? What else had she turned
her back on? Her past. Her family. She was born and raised in the

midwest. Something hardly anyone knew about her. I knew she had left Kansas City, Missouri for Harvard after high school and never looked back. Her parents were simple, down-to-earth people who didn't know how to handle a bright, too-tall, aloof loner like Shirley.

Or, maybe it was a doctor's appointment, and she was seeing a Western doctor she didn't want me to know about. Not that I expected her to see me for everything. Or anything. That would be too personal. Although she does sometimes see colleagues of mine, and of course I'd be happy to treat her in an emergency. Yes, it was probably a doctor visit.

"Dr. Watson, may I see you a moment?" She was calling me in, and I was still standing in the outer office at my mailbox, woolgathering.

"Of course."

"I was on the phone with my brother. My father is ill and I may be needed back east."

"I didn't know you had a brother."

"Mylo is my younger brother. What's important is that you may have to take over here for awhile."

"Take over?"

"The case."

"I'm not sure I'm ready. We haven't finished my training."

"I'd ask Mylo, but as this is a family emergency, we're both needed there."

"Mylo is an investigator?"

"He consults with the Kansas City Police Department."

"I see."

"I doubt it, but the critical thing is I need you to take over in my absence. Will you, or must I call in someone from New York?"

"I will. In fact, I knew you were talking on the phone with your family."

"Did you?"

"You shut your office door and turned your back on me. I deduced you were speaking with family."

"Or..."

"Okay, or your doctor, but I thought of your family first."

"Good. I'll be a phone call away. I'll take my computer, of course. Use e-mail, send photos and voice files. Record everything. Be in constant contact."

"I hope your father gets well quickly."

"He's dying. I'm going back for the funeral."

"I'm so sorry."

"Please keep it to yourself, will you Mary? Lix doesn't need to know. Tell the police I had urgent business. Tell our clients I'm investigating leads out of town. You can handle this."

"I will, Shirley. You can count on me."

Shirley put a few items in her briefcase, told Lix I was in charge of the case, and left. On the streetcar on her way to her loft, she texted me the numbers of her parents' landline, Mylo's cell phone number, his landline, and emailed me her flight itinerary. I texted back my offer to drive her to the airport. I was rebuffed and reminded of how much I had to do here and how quickly she could get to the airport on Max.

I felt as if I were standing on a ledge twenty stories up. With no one to talk me down, I had to either fly or fail. What was I afraid of? If the PPB did their job, they would solve the case without my help anyway. I wasn't alone here. Besides, Shirley was only a phone call away. This was an opportunity for me to show her what I'd learned by working with her.

I started by showing up for the arraignments and apologizing for Shirley's absence. Oceane decided she wanted to keep Hala for herself, so Ms. Cumfer referred M. Beaudet to a colleague. Both Oceane and her father were released on exorbitant bail. Lix had secured a luxurious condo on the east side of the river for them to hide away, where they were less likely to be hounded by paparazzi. She was waiting in a taxi outside the jurors' entrance for us, and whisked them away.

With Oceane and her father safely out of the clutches of the police, and Shirley on her way to the midwest, I went over what I knew for sure: Oceane was not the murderer. I was as sure of her as I was Shirley. Oceane had been willing and ready to give up her career to take care of Zaro for as long as it took. She might one day have felt like murdering Zaro, but not yet. As for her father, I wasn't so sure. He wanted to protect Zaro. Maybe he had flown into town, found Zaro alone in her room and had taken advantage of the situation. I didn't know how he would have got into her room unnoticed, and I had no idea yet how Zaro's equipment had been disabled without sounding an alarm. Still, M. Beaudet went on my list of suspects. Bori, of course, still ranked number one. And I couldn't help being suspicious of cousin Khalil, though I questioned whether I might be racist in that bias. I had to look closely at all the facts on each person. Shirley always made it clear that all personal bias must be kept out of the process. Easy to say, not so easy to do.

Khalil was Zaro's blood relative, but he was also her employee. She was the one with all the money. Did he resent reporting to her? Watching her be able to buy anything, do anything, go anywhere she pleased? In their home culture, it was all well and good for a girl child to assume a male identity up to a point. When they reached marrying age, they were expected to return to their female identities and behave accordingly. Zaro hadn't. She was a woman who had grown up with male privilege, and never relinquished it. She maintained her privilege by fighting tooth and nail for her independence, by being smarter, more driven than others, rising to the top of her chosen profession in spite of her gender. All this despite her sexuality, I couldn't omit that fact. She had supported the Mujahedeen in the fight against Soviet occupation, operating as an informant and organizing supplies of food, medicine and even weapons, during the ten year occupation.

She had grown up as a boy, a young man. She was independent, she was educated as a boy. She had the rights and responsibilities of a man. And when it came time for her to assume the role and responsibilities of a woman, she would not do it, had no desire to do it.

Zaro left Kandahar when the Russians left Afghanistan. She emigrated to Denmark, and quickly made a fortune in investments by day trading. It was just before the bubble burst, and she invested wisely. Somewhere along the way, she also discovered that she was attracted to women, and with her freedom, her newfound wealth, she could have women as well. She made friends in the wealthy social set and began to travel the world, as she could look after her investments via computer from anywhere. She bought a yacht for her primary residence and kept her money in Swiss bank accounts.

What had happened with her familial relationships once Zaro left Kandahar? All we knew for certain was Khalil had come to work for her. I asked Lix to see what else she could find out.

Bori had been the police's prime suspect with good reason. She was the person who shot acid into Zaro's face and put her into the hospital. The question for all the suspects, except Oceane, was: how could they have got into Zaro's room, put the overdose into her IV, and disabled the equipment without notice? For Oceane it was only the equipment question, because she could get in, could have injected the morphine, and got back out without raising suspicion among the staff—if they had seen her.

While Lix was looking into Khalil in more depth, I decided to dig a bit deeper into Bori's past and present. I started with the internet, of course. The problem is one has to be careful about the information found there. Wikipedia can't be trusted. Anything published by newspapers has to be taken with a grain of salt. But court records, vital records, those are obtainable and neither fiction nor subject to rewriting.

I double-checked all the records Lix had collected regarding Bori's travel from the East Coast to Portland. Bori wasn't obvious, she first went to a Lipizzaner show and sale in New York, and flew to Las Vegas on Jet Blue. From there she borrowed a car and told people she was going to Yosemite.

She actually drove to Portland, stopping at cheap motels along the way, paying cash, turning off the GPS in the car, in her phone, buying burner phones, buying VISA debit cards to use in case the motel wanted a credit card up front. Lix was able to unearth the fact that Bori bought Hydrochloric Acid (spirits of salt) in a Las Vegas hardware store in the cleaning supply area. In Portland at Walmart, she bought several squirt guns, and the right kind of gloves to wear when cleaning to remove rust. She wore disguises for these tasks, but used her VISA debit cards. Obviously she thought by buying debit cards they wouldn't be traceable. She made the mistake of buying the cards the same place she bought the package of burner phones, and she was remembered because of her looks and her accent. Even in a black wig, she was gorgeous and bore a striking resemblance to Uma Thurman in *Kill Bill*.

From public records in Hungary, I learned that Bori was the daughter of Lipizzan horse farmers in Bana. The Esztis owned a large number of mares, raised the horses and sold the colts. Both her parents had been arrested in 1989 during the anti-Soviet rallies. They may have taken her and her siblings along when the barbed wire came down that summer. Although the farm would have been busy, her parents were still young enough and radical enough to participate. Hungarians, as a culture, tend to be hot-blooded, brainy, and good-looking. The Hungarians invented many things including the atomic bomb, the hydrogen bomb, and were instrumental in the nuclear bomb as well. The Esztis were educated, intelligent people, and Bori was apparently one of the hot-headed ones. Hot-headed and cold-blooded enough to plan her acid attack on Zaro and carry it out. Had she also murdered her in her bed? She had no police record, in the United States or abroad, until now. She was thirty years old, a grown woman. According to her FaceBook page, she had had a number of affairs with women in the past ten years. None of them had been long lasting. She seemed to have fallen hardest for Zaro. According to Bori, she broke off the affair after learning that Zaro had killed her previous fiancée.

We needed to find out how the hospital equipment had been dismantled so successfully. That mystery was impeding solution to the murder itself. I had searched the internet without success. It looked like I was going to have to employ Shirley's methods: go in person and figure it out. I didn't have a search warrant, but why would I need one? I needn't even go to OHSU to solve this. I would go to a medical equipment supply house. There was one across the river on the southeast side.

The HealthCare supply place was a warehouse near the OMSI Museum. I entered the reception area, showed my medical credentials to the aging receptionist whose black plastic nameplate identified as Gary Hope. I asked him to show me the type of patient monitoring equipment one might need for a patient recovering from burns. He called a sales rep. I hoped this wasn't going to be a hard sell from an eager rep. A woman about my own age came up within ninety seconds or so, wearing a navy pantsuit with a creamy silk blouse. Her glasses matched the blouse, and her black hair had a streak of dark blue that nearly matched the pantsuit. Her bangs were so long they fell below the top of her glasses frames. Her eyes might have been brown, or even dark blue. Her teeth sparkled as though she'd just come from a bleaching treatment at the dentist.

"What can I show you today, doctor?"

"Hi. I'm Dr. Watson. And you are?" I wasn't going to be whisked away without even an introduction.

"Oh, sorry. I'm Beth Adams."

"Beth Adams? The same one who sells real estate?"

"Guilty as charged. The market has been slow, and HealthCare was kind enough to offer me a full time position here. Have we met?"

"No, I saw your name on a sign."

"You house-hunting?"

"No, no, I don't know, maybe. For some reason your name stuck with me."

"Great, doctor, how can I help you?"

"I need to look at patient monitoring equipment."

She began telling me about all the types of monitoring equipment they had on hand as she led me into the sales room. I quickly came clean with her and told her what I actually needed, and let her know I wasn't going to buy any equipment.

"That's okay, I'm happy to help you. Who knows? Maybe next time you buy something for your practice, you'll come back here."

"Thank you, Beth. And call me Mary. I appreciate your help, and I will definitely come here next time I need something for the practice."

Beth showed me several monitoring systems, but none of them looked the same as I'd seen in Zaro's hospital room until we got to the Carescape B850. This one had all the bells and whistles. As it should, it was the most expensive monitor on the floor. Beth showed me the plug, and explained that this type of equipment required a different type of electrical wiring, precisely so it could not be accidentally unplugged. Trying to pull this plug from the wall while the monitor was running would result in a shock at the least.

"What happens to this unit when the patient's heart stops?"

"Alarms go off, both locally at the bedside, and at the nurses' station."

"Would it ever be the case that the alarms could go unnoticed?"

"Well, this does have one unique feature. It can be programmed to alarm however you want it to."

"Including not at all?"

"Theoretically. Although no hospital would do that. They might program it not to go off in the patient's room, so as not to disturb the patient or his or her guests in case of a malfunction, but they would still want to be aware of it at the nurses' station."

"But it's possible?"

"It's possible, but why would you want that?"

"Not for any good reason I can think of." With that, I had all I needed. Still, I decided to invite Beth out for a coffee break, if she had time.

She did. We walked over to Cooper's Coffee House. We chatted a bit about the monitor. I wanted in the worst way to learn how to program it, but training on the equipment came from the different manufacturers. That wasn't going to happen. So we turned to talking about houses. I confessed I'd seen her name in conjunction with a bungalow not too far from where we were sipping our lattes. She offered to take me through it after work if I wanted.

What could it hurt? I wasn't going to buy a house, but maybe Beth and I would become friends. She had the most pleasant laugh. And she was wearing a rainbow pin on her lapel.

Chapter Twelve:
A Night to Remember

As Beth Adams and I walked through the bungalow in southeast Portland, I listened to her describe the bedrooms, the built-ins in the dining room and kitchen, the beautiful leaded glass windows in the living room and front door, and instead of imagining myself living there alone—or more sensibly, just nodding along—I envisioned myself living there with my wife. I could even imagine a child or two clambering up and down the stairs. In the kitchen as Beth pointed out the gas range, dishwasher and black soapstone countertops (I loved those!) I found myself imagining laughing with her over a dinner we had prepared together. I had to shake myself and dash out the back door for fresh air. The backyard was exactly the right size, fenced in with a good neighbor fence six feet high, and filled with Oregon native trees, bushes and flowers.

Beth reeled off the benefits of xeriscaping already put in, remarked on the handy (also handsome) outbuilding for gardening tools. I noticed the shed also had a large window. It could be a studio or writer's retreat for someone who had a family.

I thanked Beth for the showing and took the sell sheet. I was shaken to my core by the fantasies that had taken hold of me in that house. All my life, since puberty anyway, I assumed I was asexual. That had been one of the major attractions I had to Shirley. She clearly had no interest in forming a sexual bond with anyone. Her confidence in that aspect of herself affirmed my own. Now here I was, feeling not only a "crush" on a woman, but fantasizing about being married to one. I supposed I was allowing that fantasy in light of all the states now allowing marriage between two people of the same sex. Maybe it was companionship I was missing? Still, I was definitely feeling the crush on Beth. I loved her voice, the way her eyes crinkled when she smiled, and her habit of placing her hand on mine when she was enthusiastic about something.

I knew I wanted to see her again. I also wanted that house. I knew I wanted to sit on its back deck and watch little Martha kitty explore the backyard. I looked over the sell sheet again. The price was right. Portland bungalows don't usually stay on the market long. I liked the neighborhood, and it was close enough to downtown I could walk or ride my bike to the office. I pulled the car over and called Beth to ask her to meet me later so we could place an offer on the house.

I drove to the office and typed up my report on the Carescape B850 monitor. I had plenty of time before my meeting with Beth to think about who might have reprogrammed the monitor. Our killer would have to have had access to Zaro's monitor or one like it prior to killing her. He or she would have had to have access to the actual monitor in order to reprogram it on the night of her death. I wondered how long it would take a person to learn how to do the programming if they weren't familiar with it? I decided to ask Beth if she'd let me experiment on the equipment at HealthCare—without supervision, and without manuals.

At the office, Shirley called. I gave her my update. She wanted an update from Oceane, M. Beaudet, Khalil, and Bori by the end of the day. I asked about her father. He was still dying, not yet gone. I asked about the rest of her family, but she gave me the brush off and said she'd call daily for updates. I wanted to ask her if she had thoughts or ideas about our suspects, but I knew she wouldn't speculate. I also knew if she had anything she wanted to share with me regarding our case, she would. So I saved my breath.

I checked in with Lix after the call to tell her what Shirley's expectations were and asked her to update my electronic calendar so I wouldn't neglect to write out the necessary reports. The alert I would receive would also help me prepare for Shirley's daily calls.

Lix had learned a little more about Zaro's background since the day before. She had compiled a list of women Zaro had been paired with, sometimes for a few days, sometimes weeks, and occasionally a bit longer. The list included the woman she had killed, followed by Bori, two more short term women, and finally Oceane. I asked Lix to obtain addresses and telephone numbers for the last ten on the list. Lix also found out Zaro had hired her father's brother's son (Khalil) about the same time she bought the yacht. And that "ibn" as Zaro and Khalil called each other is translated simply "cousin."

I decided to contact the women on the list of ten, not including Bori and Oceane, to see whether they could give me any insights on why Zaro was murdered. Meanwhile, I wanted to check in with Beth to see how her day was going. In my entire adult life, I hadn't had that many crushes. I wondered whether my hormones were surging now or whether something was out of whack in my system. I'd never had a big sex drive, in fact it was nearly non-existent. Was this what was known as the "ticking biological clock?" I was at the age a lot of women decide to nest and have babies. Was my fantasizing about having a wife nothing more than my clock ticking? I didn't want to bear any babies. I decided that when I was a toddler. My grandmother often reminded me of the time when she tried to buy me a doll, and I said to her "how many times do I have to tell you? I don't like babies!" I was four years old at the time. Now, I was about to achieve my thirty-fifth birthday. Shirley celebrated her fortieth by ignoring it and refusing to allow me or Lix to acknowledge. Thirty-five is about the time most people begin their mid-life crisis, or so I'd read. Maybe that was why I was having these notions of marriage and living with someone. Beth. But what if I'd been wrong about being asexual, and I was a late bloomer? That was possible.

Rather than drive myself crazy with my circular thinking, I decided to act on my feelings. I called Beth. My heart seemed to be pounding on my sternum, my breathing was shallow, and my ears were ringing, but I managed to say—through a dry throat—that I wanted to have dinner together.

"You need more information about the monitor?"

"No, I…"

"Oh, about the house! Wonderful, I'll meet you…"

"I'd like to pick you up, Beth. I'm asking you on a date."

"Well, that's different."

"Does that mean no?"

"Not at all. It means I need time to get out of my work clothes and into something suitable for a date. What time do you want to come by?"

"I'll make reservations for 8. And I'll be at your place at 7:30."

She gave me her home address, and I rang off. I had to get a drink of water, and wipe off my damp palms, before I could get back to work. My phone rang. It was Beth.

"So does this mean our meeting this afternoon is off? Or are we going to talk about the house tonight?"

"Oh no! I completely forgot our meeting. I was so excited to ask you for a date…"

She laughed. "That's okay, I just need to know."

"Maybe we'd better go ahead with our meeting. I don't want to lose my chance at getting the house."

"I'll have all the paperwork with me. So, great! I get to see you twice today. You might turn out to be my favorite client."

"You never know." What a dork I was. I was trying to be suave, but I sounded like a dweeb to my own ears. Somehow we managed to complete the call, and I once again wiped my palms on my pants, took a swig of water, and this time I returned to work.

Lix gave me the addresses and phone numbers she had managed to gather so far, and I made the telephone calls. I reached three voicemails before I got an answer. Of course, it was already evening in Europe, where most of the women were located.

"*Bonsoir.*"

"Hello, this is Dr. Mary Watson calling from the United States. May I speak with Julienne Behr, please?"

"This is Julienne. *Parlez-vous français?*"

"*Non,* I'm sorry. Do you speak English?"

"A little. Why is a doctor calling, *s'il vous plaît?*"

"I'm investigating a murder, Mademoiselle, and I hoped would you answer some questions for me about Zaro Sadozai."

"Has she killed someone?"

"I'm sorry to tell you that it is Ms. Sadozai who has been killed."

"Ha! Where has this taken place? You are calling from the United States?"

"Yes, it happened here in Portland, Oregon, the northwest part of the country."

"How?"

"May I ask you some questions about Ms. Sadozai before we get into that?"

"*Oui,* but of course."

"Thank you. When were you and she, uh, going together?"

"We were lovers for a short time. Maybe three months. It was almost five years ago."

"So before she was accused of killing Dody Pearce."

"*Oui.* Zaro left me for another woman, not Dody. I don't remember her name, but she was German. Zaro always loves them and leaves them. Or in Dody's case, perhaps she killed her."

"Do you believe Zaro killed Dody Pearce?"

"Zaro is ... was capable of causing great pain and much suffering for women. I believe she killed men when she was working for the Mujahadeen."

"During the Afghan war?"

"Of course. But Zaro continued to carry that cold blood even after. I do think she killed Dody. I think she could kill anyone. I was heart broken when she left me, until I got my senses back. I thought I was lucky."

"Did she ever physically harm you?"

"Zaro didn't consider what she did as harmful or painful. But I can tell you it was."

"What do you mean?"

"She liked the how you call it? S and M."

"S and M sex. Did she use instruments? Paddles or whips?"

"*Non.* She liked to tie me down and choke me until I lost consciousness."

"Do you know whether this was something she did with other women?"

"She told me that all her women enjoyed this type of sex, and I should too. I wanted to be with her, so I let her do what she liked."

Many people enjoy S and M without hurting anyone. "Didn't you have a safe word?"

"I wasn't allowed to speak during this type of sex. So, no. There were no 'safe words' or any words at all, on my part."

"What about Zaro, did she say anything?"

"She liked to say that she could kill me and no one would ever know. That is why I was so frightened, once I was free of her. When I was with her, it was as if I were under her spell. Afterwards, I never wanted to see her again. As I said, I counted myself lucky."

"Did you testify at her trial?"

"No one asked me. I don't think I could have. I was afraid to even look at her pictures."

"Why was that?"

"When I look at her pictures, I still want her. It makes me feel ashamed. I could not have sat in the same courtroom with her and accused her of anything."

"Where did you meet her?"

"At a party, here in Paris. You might say it was love at first sight. She asked me to dance, and once I was in her arms, I belonged to her and no one else. Not for those three months we were together, anyway. I don't know how long I might have stayed if she hadn't left me."

"Have you communicated with her at all in the years since you broke up?"

"I sent her a few letters when she first left. But once I came back to myself, never. She never wrote or called or contacted me at all. It was as if I had never existed for her."

"Thank you so much for your time, Julienne."

"Have my answers helped you?"

"Yes, yes they have. If you think of anything else you want to tell me, please call me any time."

I gave her my numbers, both at the office and my cell. Her story made me think. I'd never given much thought to S and M sex, though I'd read about it. My philosophy has always been that consenting adults should do whatever pleased them. But this wasn't the kind of sex I had read about. What little I knew of S and M was the safe word concept where the participants could call out that word and whatever was in progress had to come to a stop. What Zaro was doing to Julienne was not that. It was abusive, even though Julienne hadn't said no at the time.

What if Beth was into bondage and all that? Would I be interested? Talk about jumping ahead. We hadn't even had our first date yet. I was so unpolished I wouldn't even know how to make the first move toward a kiss, let alone sex of any kind. Maybe she would be the one to attempt to kiss me. Did I want that?

My head would not stop its carousel of delights. I pictured us laughing across the table, kissing in the moonlight, even undressing in my house. My house? Tonight? No way was I prepared for sex on a first date. I couldn't take her to my home. No. We would eat dinner, and I would take her home and say goodnight. That would be enough for the first time.

After I made a few more calls to Zaro's former lovers, left a few more voicemail messages, it was too late to call overseas any longer. I checked in with our client, made sure she was being taken care of, and I sat back in my chair and allowed myself to daydream about that Portland bungalow in southeast Portland. Finally it was time for my meeting with Beth. I rushed off to our agreed upon place— Cooper's. Beth was waiting for me at a back table, papers spread out, pen in hand.

Beth showed me the comparable listings with prices, told me how long the house had been on the market, showed me an array of photos of the place, even though I'd looked at it, and suggested an opening bid. She wanted to go in a few thousand dollars less than the asking price, but I wanted the house, so I placed a bid for the full price, the only conditions being my loan approval and the full inspection of the property. I offered several thousand dollars in earnest money. I knew I could get a loan, because I had enough saved to pay cash. But that wouldn't be the best use of my money, so I wasn't going to do it. I would, however, put twenty percent down because I had no intention of paying for mortgage insurance every month on top of the principal, interest and homeowner's insurance. The interest on the house would be tax deductible, so buying a home was a good way to increase my net worth at the same time I decreased my tax liability. Why hadn't I done this before? Beth assured me that I was buying a house at exactly the right time. The market was going to turn around, and my property would begin to increase its worth over time. She was so smart. I liked that about her.

Once I'd completed the paperwork and written the check, Beth called the homeowners and gave them my offer. They accepted immediately. That made me wonder whether I should have offered less. Too late now. Now it was hire the inspector, and move on to the next step.

We toasted my win with lattes, and Beth left to do the rest of the paperwork. She would fax the signed agreements to me at my home.

We said so long for the time being. I called Lix from my parked car and told her I was gone for the day. She would let me know if Shirley or any of our clients needed me. I drove home imagining myself in every outfit in my closet. What was I going to wear on my honest-to-goodness first date? Maybe I should go shopping? No. Everything I owned would be new to Beth except for what I wore yesterday and today. I had to pull over and make more phone calls when I realized I hadn't actually made dinner reservations. After a few fails, I was finally able to reserve a table for two at a new Italian place I'd heard of, but not been to, on southeast Division. Beth lived in the southeast as well, so we wouldn't have far to travel. That was good because I didn't know how I was going to keep my eyes on the road with her sitting beside me.

This was going to be a night to remember.

Chapter Thirteen:
First Date

WHEN I ARRIVED AT BETH'S HOUSE TO PICK HER UP, SHE was sitting on the front porch. Her house had all the curb appeal it should have, given her profession as a realtor, but I barely glanced at it. My eyes were on Beth. I felt my heart speed up as I started up the walk. Our eyes met, and Beth broke into a smile that showed off her perfect teeth and crinkled her eyes. My own face was wreathed in a broad grin, and I could feel a flush on my neck and cheeks. How could I be this happy to meet someone I hardly knew? I felt deranged, completely out of control.

Somehow I managed to drive to the restaurant without crashing into anyone. It was the epitome of "distracted driving." Portland drivers and pedestrians got off lucky that time. I went around to open her car door, but Beth was already standing on the sidewalk waiting for me. Inside the restaurant, I made to pull her chair out for her, but once again she was ahead of me. I pulled out my own chair and sat down as the server looked on us with a smile. I couldn't tell what he was thinking, but my attempt to seat my date hadn't gone unnoticed. He asked me what kind of wine we would like, brought it to me for my approval, and I knew he was going to bring me the check as well. I was feeling pretty butch. All of a sudden I felt pressured. If I were butch, wouldn't I have to play all the male roles? Yes,

I'd been a tomboy as a youngster, but I had no desire to either be a man or act like one. Okay, I was going to have to slow down. Take this whole thing slow. For one thing, I needed to do some research. Read about lesbians, what they do, what the expectations are. So for this night, I would try to be myself, and whatever happened—well, it would happen.

The menu was in Italian, but not that difficult to decipher. We had some tasty local veggies, and pasta, followed by dessert. I tried the anneloni with chanterelles and chilis for my pasta, and Beth had rigatoni with zucchini pesto. For dessert we split a hazelnut semifreddo. The wine was terredora di paolo "rosaenovae" and completely suitable for a celebration of my getting a house. Which is about how often I drink. So after two glasses, I was buzzed, and pretty certain my alcohol level was above Oregon's legal limit. When we left the restaurant, I suggested a long walk. We trekked over to Laurelhurst Park, sat by the duck pond until it was almost dark, and strolled back to my car. By that time, I was totally sober, and even more entranced by Beth.

We shared stories of our childhood, swapped family information, and discussed my new house. Beth was a wealth of details about what happens in the process, and filled me in as the first time buyer I was. She referred to me as a "virgin," never dreaming that I was not only a virgin homeowner, but one who still had her hymen.

As I drove her home I finally asked her whether she was involved with anyone.

"Not at the moment. My ex and I broke up almost two years ago, and I've kept busy with my two jobs. I haven't even been on a date."

"Until tonight, you mean."

"Until tonight. You were awfully bold to ask me out, you know that?"

"I want to get to know you better. I can't keep buying houses in order to see you."

She threw back her head and laughed out loud at that. She reached for my hand. I took it off the wheel, and gave it to her. As we pulled up in front of her house, I had barely turned off the engine when she put her arm around my neck and pulled my face to hers. She kissed me eagerly and teased my lips apart with her tongue. I felt a hot tingling in places I hadn't felt tingling before. Not like this. I pulled back to catch my breath.

"Do you want to come inside?" Her voice was almost a whisper.

"I, I have to get home. I have work to do yet tonight. Can I get a raincheck?"

"If you must, doctor."

"Are you free on Friday night?" That would give me a couple of days to do my research and pull myself together.

"Nothing I can't reschedule. What time?"

"Maybe earlier?"

"Let's go to a movie, and we'll come back here for coffee."

"Sounds great. You choose the movie and I'll be here whatever time you say."

She agreed to the plan, and kissed me again. My heart was pounding, my breathing was shallow, and I felt quite sticky between my thighs. I watched as she walked up the path and stairs to her house. I waited until she was safely inside before driving myself home. What a long drive Lake Oswego seemed, suddenly. But soon I'd be living in this neighborhood, only a few streets over from Beth. When I got inside my house, I picked up Martha and danced around the living room.

I felt so happy I couldn't sleep all night. When the sun came up about five a.m., I got up and danced again. Martha refused to join me. She wanted breakfast instead. As for me, I had no appetite. I was wired. Was this what love felt like? It had to be infatuation. No one could fall in love that quickly.

I didn't have to be in the office for a couple of hours, so I got online and started my lesbian related research. What did people do before the internet? I quickly learned there was no need for me to be concerned about roles, because lesbians did their relationships however they wanted. Yes there were couples who did the butch/ femme thing, but apparently even there one didn't have to strictly comply to the male/female roles created by society. There was a full spectrum of types of relationships. Femme/femme, butch/butch, androgynous for one or both, and everything in between. Basically the "rule" was: be yourself. If you find each other and you want to be together, the two of you decide how you want it. So complicated!

It would be up to me to decide whether I wanted to pursue a relationship with Beth, and up to her to decide if she wanted one with me. Meanwhile, I had another date, and the strong feeling that Beth would expect sex as part of that date. Did I want that? My body did. I was flooded with fear of failure. I didn't know anything about making love. With Beth or anyone else.

I typed in "lesbian sex," and was sorry I had. My screen was filled with pornographic links and scenes. I decided to take my research offline. I would go to the women's bookstore after work and get some books.

I forced myself to eat a bowl of cereal with blueberries. I drove to the office. I didn't need coffee today, not yet anyway. Even without sleep I felt as if I'd had eight cups of coffee already. I couldn't sit still. Even on the telephone, I had to get up and pace back and forth beside my desk as I left messages. Finally, I reached a live person.

"Patricia Gillies please."

"This is Trish. Who's calling?"

"You don't know me, Ms. Gillies. My name is Dr. Mary Watson, and I'm investigating the Zaro Sadozai case. You used to date Ms. Sadozai, isn't that right?"

"What case? What are you talking about? I thought Zaro was found not guilty."

"I'm sorry to tell you that Ms. Sadozai has been killed."

"Killed? In an accident?"

"Killed in suspicious circumstances, I'm afraid."

"What does this have to do with me?"

"We're trying to learn more about Zaro Sadozai herself. And as you once dated her, I thought you might be able to tell me more about her. If you're willing."

"Where did you say you are?"

"I didn't. I'm in Portland, Oregon. In the US."

"Oregon? Zaro died in Oregon?"

"That's right. She was here for Rose Festival."

"In her yacht?"

"Right."

"And someone murdered her?"

"Someone did."

"You want to know why. Why someone would want to kill a rich woman."

"Yes, basically." I could hear the bitterness in Trish's voice.

"Probably whoever stands to inherit her money."

"We're looking into that."

"Well maybe you should look into whoever she was dating at the time. Zaro could be a real bitch."

"How so?"

"Anyway you can think of, Dr. Watson. Zaro could stab you in the heart with one or two words. She had a knack of learning where you were most vulnerable, and using that against you. If the last thing you wanted was to have some secret revealed, she'd be sure to bring it up as a party topic, and laugh at you while you squirmed in embarrassment."

"That sounds horrible."

"Yeah. It was."

"What else?"

"That's not enough?"

"Would you kill someone for it?"

"I didn't. She did that to me more than once, and yet I didn't kill her. Amazing, isn't it? There was something about her. It was like being addicted to heroin. I wanted her bad enough to stick around even after she tore my heart out with that shit."

"So she left you?"

"Yes, she dumped me. Found herself another victim. One after another, that was her style. I think she got tired of women after she humiliated them and they didn't stand up for themselves. You know she killed one, right?"

"We know about Dody, yes."

"Even after that, women still continue to fall for her charms."

"Did you ever try to get back with her?"

"Only right after she dumped me. But I could see it wasn't going to happen. She looked at me like I was of no interest to her at all. I could have been yesterday's newspaper for all I mattered to her. My blood ran cold. I never saw her again after that one time. To tell you the truth, it scared me."

"You were scared of Zaro?"

"Not when we were together, but when she looked at me with those cold dead eyes, the hair on the back of my neck stood up. I had the feeling that if I bothered her again she might kill me. And when I heard she'd killed Dody, I knew I was right."

"But she never hit you?"

"She never laid a hand on me. She didn't have to, she had me completely under her thumb."

"Thank you so much for this, Trish. Is there anything else you want to tell me about Zaro?"

"You know she wanted to be a man, right?"

"As in sex change?"

"I don't know about that. I just know that after she spent all that time pretending to be a boy, she hated being a woman."

I left her with my phone number and e-mail in case she thought of anything else she wanted to share. I sat thinking about the many women of Zaro Sadozai, and what her life must have been like pretending to be a boy. Not for a few minutes, not cross-dressing once and trying it out, but year after year as her father's son, in order to fool the Afghani government. She grew up with the rights and responsibilities of a boy. She got educated, trained in weapons, and fought alongside her father and other men. I could think about it, but I couldn't imagine it. I had stood on the side of the bathtub once and pulled my hair back, staring at my face in the mirror, thinking "this is what I would look like if I were a boy." I had complained about the injustice of being a girl in a man's world. But I simply could not imagine what Zaro's life had been. And how could her father expect her to suddenly become a woman, act like an Afghani woman with all that meant? I didn't blame her for resisting, leaving her home, her country, and starting over.

How had her life led to her death? That wasn't so hard to see. It seemed to me that any of the women she'd ever dated could have tracked her down and killed her. But why here? Why now? It had to be Bori. Who else had that kind of motive? Of course, that's never the only motive for murder. Love is merely the top motive. Money—another popular motive. And in this case, there was plenty of money. Who stood to gain Zaro's estate?

I went to lunch, and when I got back, Lix was waiting for me, practically jumping up and down with excitement.

"Mary, Mary, I found out more about Zaro and her family!"

"Don't keep me waiting, Lix. Spill."

"First of all, everything was not so hunky-dory between Zaro and her cousin Khalil. She hired him okay, but he was a resentful dick who thought she should die in an honor killing."

"Whoa! Where did you get this information?"

"From his MySpace page."

"You mean FaceBook?"

"No, he doesn't use the MySpace page anymore, but his posts are still up from back when he was writing about his "shemale" cousin. Don't you hate it when people use that term?"

"What did he say exactly?"

"Here are the printouts. I made screen copies so you could see the whole thing."

"This is great, Lix. Anything else?"

"Like that's not enough? But okay, there is more."

"Good going. Whatcha got?"

"Zaro's will. I dug until I found out the name of her lawyer, and I got him to fax a copy of her most recent will."

"Hallelujah! Let me see."

"I was hoping you'd bring me a coffee on your way back from lunch."

"I have to get you coffee before you hand me the will?"

"No. It would have been nice is all."

"Here. Take my coffee card and go get whatever you want."

"You want anything?"

"No, I'm good."

"There's cold water in the fridge. And some homemade lemonade if you want it."

"Go! I can't wait to read these documents!"

Lix skipped out and I hurried to my desk where I have a lamp. I find that the right lighting helps everything, especially reading documents. Mine has a magnifier too for the small print. I don't like overhead lighting except in the kitchen, and even there I like lighting under the cabinets. Oh! Does my new house have that kind of task lighting? I forgot to notice.

Khalil Sadozai's MySpace page was deplorable. I checked the photos to make sure I was looking at the right guy. Maybe he'd changed in the few years since his last posting, or maybe he was hiding his true personality now. Back then he made racist, homophobic, misogynistic remarks in almost every post. In one post, prior to Zaro's hiring him, he said believed in honor killings and had a cousin who should be a candidate because she refused to accept her "rightful place" as a bride and mother. I was hoping he meant another cousin, but he said this cousin was sapphic. He defined sapphic in words I refused to repeat. How many lesbian cousins who refused to accept their role as women could he have? He had to mean Zaro.

Next came the will. It was far from simple. Zaro had thousands of assets to be sorted out. She left a foundation for her favorite charity in Afghanistan, one which educated girls. She bequeathed individual items to each of the women on my contact list, including Bori. Plus almost ninety more. Then came the part of her will that caused me to gasp and spit out my sip of water: To my blood relatives, I leave nothing, except for my half-brother, Khalil Sarozai, whom I trust with my life. Khalil and I grew up believing we were cousins, but I have learned that in fact, he is my father's son, just as I am my father's daughter. Khalil's mother is my father's sister-in-law, my uncle's second wife. He is the only sibling who has ever acknowledged me for who I am, and as such I leave him all my personal goods and possessions. In addition, a trust must be established to provide him with income for life from all my holdings that are not dedicated to my foundation.

Holy Batman. Khalil would inherit millions, plus the yacht, her real estate, all vehicles, everything right down to her sandals, everything not otherwise bequeathed.

I moved Khalil to the top of my suspect list. I called the PPB immediately. Lt. Xio was not in the office. I asked for the lead detective on the Zaro Sadozai case, and was informed that Lt. Xio was heading up the task force himself. I was welcome to leave a voicemail. So I did. I called Shirley.

"I'm sorry to bother you, Shirley, but we've turned up some new information, and I thought you'd want to know."

"That's fine. My father died half an hour ago. I can talk now."

"Oh, Shirley, I'm so sorry for your loss…"

"Never mind that. What have you learned?"

I gave her all the new information I had, starting with the will and going backwards. She was mostly silent, taking it all in. I knew she would interrupt me if she had questions, or wasn't able to hear me. I was on a landline, but I was calling her cell. Static was nearly unavoidable, but we had a clear line.

"I'll be on the next plane."

"What about the funeral? And your Mom, don't you want to stay there for your Mom?"

"I'll text you my arrival time as soon as I have it. Please meet me. We have work to do."

She rung off without answering my questions, and I began preparing to answer the questions she would have upon arrival.

CHAPTER FOURTEEN:
IN OTHER WORDS

S HIRLEY TEXTED ME. SHE WOULD GET IN AT 9:24 P.M. IF her flight was on time. Flights coming from the east are often early, so I planned to park in the cell phone lot until her plane touched down. Then she'd call and I would meet her in the departures area on the upper level. This way we would avoid the traffic jam at arrivals as everyone else waited for her or his passenger.

Meanwhile, I had time to go to In Other Words bookstore to buy some books on lesbian sex. This was one area where I didn't want to just be myself. I was too ignorant on the mechanics. I tried to focus on my driving on the way there. I found it easier to concentrate if I practiced being in the moment. I talked to myself: I feel the back of my legs on the seat. My hands are on the steering wheel. Now I'm braking for the upcoming light.

Once there, I found a parking spot, and headed inside. I wasn't a stranger here, but this would be my first time buying books on this particular subject. I'd been a supporter of In Other Words for years. When the shop was on Hawthorne Boulevard I'd attended readings, bought books and magazines, even bought a few CDs. Since the shop moved to the northeast quadrant, the drive was farther and I hadn't gone as often. But for this purpose, there wasn't another bookstore I'd even consider.

The young woman with blue hair and face jewelry greeted me as I opened the door. Her friendliness put me at ease immediately and I asked her to direct me to the books on lesbian sex. She did so cheerfully.

"Is there a particular kind of sex you're interested in?"

"No, I'm interested in all of it. I need some books on my shelf, that's all."

"We have plenty for sale. There are the new ones, of course, but if you're rounding out your collection, you might want to look on our used books shelf. Someone brought in a copy of Marilyn Gayle's 'What Lesbians Do' are you familiar with that one?"

I wasn't familiar with any of them. And Gayle's book was apparently a collectors' item, so it didn't come cheap. It was the size of a fat coloring book, with a gorgeous cover in deep red and cream, a drawing by Gayle herself. I bought it without hesitation. And I explored the new books. I recognized some of the authors' names. I had shelves of feminist nonfiction, and shouldn't have been surprised to see some of the writers names on the works I was buying today. It was only that as a practicing asexual, I didn't place importance on an author's sexual orientation. I hadn't given it any thought one way or another until now. As I looked at the authors' photos on the backs of the books, I found myself feeling attracted to some of them.

Another new experience. And here I'd been thinking that I must feel attracted to Beth simply because she was Beth. Instead it appeared that something had awakened in me. I wanted to talk with someone about it, but I hadn't been to a counselor since after my sister died. And that was back east. What I needed was a group of other women who were coming out late. Did such a thing even exist? That was research for another day.

I paid for my stack of books, put them in the bag I'd brought in with me, and headed for a coffee house. I could have tea, eat a scone, and read. Luckily for me, one of Portland's best coffee houses was around the corner on Albina Avenue, about eight short blocks away. I took my car in case I had to leave in a hurry to pick up Shirley. Once ensconced in a good spot, I started looking through my books.

It didn't take long for me to realize reading books on lesbian sex was having a physical affect on me. I carried my books to the car and put them in my trunk, hidden from Shirley's all-seeing eyes. And I drove to the airport to wait.

No sooner had I parked the car than the rain began. It was Rose Festival time, so of course it was raining. We wouldn't be covered in the Departures area, so I pulled out my umbrella from the door pocket to cover Shirley as she put her bag behind the front seat. This rain looked like it was going to stick around for several hours. Here in the Pacific Northwest we have several words for rain. Sprinkle, drizzle, mist, showers, downpour, deluge, and the standard rain. We don't carry umbrellas often. If it's misting or sprinkling or drizzling we might not even put up the hoods of our rain jackets. Or even wear a rain jacket. It's only water and things do dry. But in a standard rain where the drops are coming down steadily, straight down from the clouds, or at a slight angle from a breeze, say three miles per hour, and we reach for our rain jackets, and put up the hood. Umbrellas are for covering objects, like luggage, or groceries. I keep one in the car for emergencies.

While the rain pelted the windshield, I allowed myself to daydream. I imagined my date with Beth ending with us in her bed. Those few paragraphs I'd read, along with the few pictures I'd seen, enriched my fantasies. I envisioned us kissing, and lying down together. I could see my own body without clothes, but it was difficult to imagine what Beth looked like in the nude. Did she have scars or tattoos? Was she muscular? She felt strong and looked soft. I wanted to lift those bangs from her forehead, pull off her glasses and get a good look into her eyes. Would they match that blue streak in her hair? I hadn't seen them well enough yet to be sure whether they were blue, gray, green or hazel. That first kiss had given me a quick glimpse. Enough to know they weren't brown.

What would Beth see when she looked at me without my clothes? Would she find me desirable? Maybe I should get my hair cut before our date, it was kind of shaggy. And what about my body hair? I knew that a lot of women these days were shaving and waxing everything until their bodies looked like prepubescent girls. I'd only ever shaved my armpits. Would she be repelled by my pubic hair? And what if she was waxed? I'd never seen a live woman with a Brazilian or no hair at all, only pictures. I'd have to deal with it. And what of those few hairs around my nipples? Should I pluck them? I would. If she had them and didn't pluck, I'd grow mine back out. Or maybe I'd not pluck them and see if she was appalled. Other than the hair issues, I was ordinary. A few moles here and there. No scars, no tats, nothing extra like a third nipple. Small breasts, slim but wiry. Stronger than I look.

If it hadn't been raining, I'd have gotten out of the car and walked for awhile. Not distance walking, but around the lot, to stretch my legs, let off some of the excess energy. Instead, I tried to calm my mind by thinking about something else. I started naming fruits and vegetables in alphabetical order, and by the time I got to "J" I was asleep.

My phone was blaring "Help" by the Beatles for at least half a minute before I answered. Shirley had landed and was headed for the Departures area. I blinked a few times to get my eyes focused before I started the car. My head was still in the dream I'd been having. I'd been wandering from room to room in an enormous house, looking for Martha. There had been no furniture, only huge dark rooms, and I was calling and calling, "here kitty, here kitty." I had this awful feeling I'd moved house and left Martha behind. Of course it was only a nightmare. I'd never leave my cat. I hate animal peril dreams. They filled me with guilt.

I suddenly realized I hadn't told Shirley about buying a house, about meeting Beth, about my galloping hormones. Not that I shared everything with Shirley, but we'd come to have certain expectations of each other, including her expecting me to answer every beck and call.

I pulled up and jumped out of the car with my umbrella, but Shirley had put her travel bag in the back before I got to her. She was already getting into her seat as I stood there uselessly. I returned to the driver's side, got in, and welcomed her home.

"Any news to report since this afternoon?" She was all business as she looked me over in the dark. "What's wrong with you? Has something happened?"

"I fell asleep while I was waiting, that's all."

"No. You smell different. Kind of feral."

"I stink?"

"No. You don't have a bad odor, but you smell as if you ... Have you had sex?"

"No! I'm sorry if I don't smell up to par. I've been busy. I didn't have time to shower after work before I came to pick you up."

"You had time to nap."

"Okay, good grief. I was fantasizing before I fell asleep. Okay?"

"Oh, you were masturbating. Why didn't you say so? That's perfectly natural."

"I wasn't. I didn't."

"You obviously don't want to discuss it. What do you want to tell me, Mary?"

I sighed. I was having to keep a close eye on traffic as I maneuvered from the airport to I-205S to I-84W.

"I've met someone and I'm buying a house."

"You've met someone and you're buying a house? What does that mean?"

"It means I decided to buy a house, and when I met the realtor, I sort of fell for her. Her name is Beth Adams."

"All this in a matter of days. While the cat's away, eh Watson?"

"It had nothing to do with your being away, Shirl." Two could play at this game.

"I've hurt your feelings?"

"You trivialized my experience. As you well know, I've been asexual my entire life. Now I find myself attracted to this woman, and frankly it has turned my world upside down. Also, I've bought a house for the first time."

"I apologize. You're right, these are large occurrences. But you're upset about them. Or are you afraid that I am jealous?"

"I'm excited and happy about both things. But I'm a little scared about your reaction. I didn't think you'd be jealous in the sense of my having feelings for Beth instead of you, but maybe of the attention I give her, and of the time I'll be devoting to my move."

"Obviously you'll have to figure out your time, your schedule, to accommodate our work while you are closing on your house, moving and I presume simultaneously carrying on some kind of love affair with your realtor."

"I don't intend to let my work suffer."

"We never intend to. You'll have to be vigilant. Buying real estate causes daily interruptions, as you'll see. And as I've observed in others, so does dating."

"I'll do my best to keep up my work standards."

"What's our next step on the case?"

Now we had reached I-405 and were almost to her exit. I told her I needed to focus on driving until we were at her place. Once inside, we went to the dining table, pulled out tablets, iPads, and other necessary gear and went over the case from beginning to current day. We decided to question Khalil again the next day, given what we now knew about his blood relationship with Zaro. After another half an hour's discussion, I drove home to Lake Oswego.

Martha was meowing before I got the door open. Poor kitty, she was completely out of food, and had spilled her water dish. She must have been sending me telepathic notices while I was napping. I resolved to buy her a cat fountain the next time I went to the store. It wouldn't spill and she would never have to be thirsty while waiting for me to get home.

When I turned in, I took my work notes to bed with me instead of my usual novel. I wanted to be extra sharp for our Khalil interview the next morning.

CHAPTER FIFTEEN:
MY GIRLFRIEND'S BACK

WHEN LT. XIO HAD RETURNED MY CALL THE OTHER DAY, I filled him in on the details of the will. I told him that Shirley and I would interview Khalil Sadozai. At the time, Khalil was still free. By the time Shirley returned from being with her parents as her father died, Khalil was in the Justice Center on a forty-eight hour hold. The Portland Police Bureau searched the entire yacht immediately after Zaro was killed, having already searched it when she was injured. If they hadn't found anything to incriminate Khalil those two times, I didn't know what they could have found in a third search. Nevertheless, they searched again. In fact, yellow crime tape crossed the entry at the dock when Shirley and I showed up to take another look for ourselves.

We knew Khalil was safely locked up and no one lived on the yacht currently, because Oceane had moved to the same hotel as her father. No police officer stood guard onboard or beside the entry, so we both ducked under the tape and walked up the ramp. Even if someone noticed us, in broad daylight they were likely to think we were detectives working for the PPB. Still, we didn't linger in the open. We went below to Khalil's cabin. I used my picklocks to open the door. We both entered, and Shirley shut the door behind us and relocked it. We pulled out our gloves and shoe covers, and went to work. We crawled back and forth across the room, each heading the opposite way to make sure we covered every inch of the floor, the furniture, the walls, and the ceilings. We inspected the bed, and unmade it and inspected each sheet and bedcover. We checked the pillows. We took samples of hair, fibers, and anything that looked even remotely like a clue. In the bathroom we divided the space in half, and covered our own half thoroughly. It used to be that Shirley would go back over everything I'd covered in case I missed something. Now I was fully trusted, but I often double-checked myself. After we finished with Khalil's cabin, we moved above deck into Zaro's.

Here we followed the same routine as we had in Khalil's, but the cabin was much bigger. I wondered when we were going to get caught. It seemed it would be a matter of time. I couldn't believe the yacht was sitting here unguarded. Security must be on a lunch break, or perhaps the PPB was relying on dock security, and vice versa. Either way, someone was bound to show up at some point. Shirley was stashing all the evidence in her messenger bag. Almost all. Each of us had put a sample of Khalil's DNA (hair) in our pockets. Even if caught and divested of our official samples, we would still have hair to test. I put mine in my hip pocket where nothing else resided. Shirley had hers in a breast pocket of her shirt.

After a mere three and a half hours, we were packed up and walking down the ramp when two police officers were coming down the sidewalk. They saw us duck under the crime tape.

"Halt! Hold it right there. What do you two ladies think you're doing on that boat?"

"Excuse me officer, I'm Shirley Combs. I'm investigating the Zaro Sadozai case."

"Shirley Combs? You're that private eye, aren't you?"

"I'm assisting Lt. Xio."

"We haven't heard anything about that, have we Earl?"

"I think we'd better inspect her bag, Paul."

"Good thinking, Earl. I'll take that messenger bag, Ms. Combs."

"Do you have a warrant?"

"We don't need a warrant. You two were trespassing. We can take you in."

"Very well. Look in my bag if you must."

The two men took Shirley's bag, opened it and pulled out all the evidence bags. They also removed her magnifying glass, gloves, shoe covers, an apple, and her wallet. They pulled out a box of tampons, but shoved them back in the bag.

"What's all this stuff in bags? It looks like lint and dust."

"That's right. Lint and dust. I have allergies, and I was taking these samples to my doctor so I can be tested to see if I'm allergic to these things."

"Did you steal that apple from the boat?"

"No. And the magnifying glass is mine as well."

"What are you doing with these gloves and shoe covers?"

"I have allergies. I don't like to track or carry possible allergens into my apartment, so I always keep these in my bag."

"I don't see anything stolen here, Paul."

"Maybe we'd better pat them down, just in case."

The men patted us down. Fortunately Earl missed the lock picks I had in my bra. Neither of us was carrying a weapon.

"Okay, you're clean. You can go. But don't go crawling under police tape again, or we'll take you in."

"Thank you officers. I'll let Lt. Xio know you were diligent in your duties here."

They stared after us, no doubt wondering if Shirley would really speak up for them to the department head. I thought they hadn't been very diligent or they'd have checked out the yacht before letting us go. Not that they would have found anything. Still. Suppose we'd been real criminals? They were so lax. Most of the officers I'd seen from the PPB actually were conscientious about their work, and wouldn't have let us off so easy. I felt lucky to have been spared.

"Where to now, Shirley?"

"Let's leave everything in the trunk of your car, and go interview Khalil."

We walked to my car, parked in the Riverfront parking garage, unloaded our finds and my lock picks, and drove downtown to the Justice Center, where I parked on the street. The meters were all one hour in this area, so we had to limit our time or I'd have to come back and move the car. The parking patrol chalked tires, especially near the Justice Center. Buying a new timed sticker for your window wouldn't help if the patrol came back around and saw your chalked tires.

Inside, Shirley asked to interview Khalil Sadozai. He was with his attorney at the moment, so we'd have to wait. We settled into the visitors' chairs. I kept track of the time. Finally after nearly thirty minutes, we were allowed to go back and speak with Khalil.

"Mr. Sadozai, we've discovered a few things about you since the last time we spoke."

"Very well."

"For example, when Dr. Watson here obtained a copy of Zaro's will, we learned that you and she were more than cousins."

When Khalil didn't respond, Shirley continued.

"In fact, you and she were siblings."

"I am her cousin."

"Yet you shared the same father."

"If we had been raised together as siblings, I would have been honor-bound to kill her for her perverted lifestyle."

"Did you?"

"Of course not. It was her equally perverted girlfriend who refused to let her go. It wasn't my place."

"Meaning what?"

"Zaro hired me to be her valet and bodyguard. Because of her I was able to live in the style of the rich, to travel the world. She treated me as family."

"You were family. Even if you don't acknowledge the fact that you were siblings, you were cousins. She addressed you as such."

"That's correct. I had no reason to kill her."

I couldn't help interjecting, even though Shirley was leading the interview. I said, "Really? It seems to me you had several million reasons to kill her. She left you almost everything."

"I already had access to everything."

"But she could have fired you at any time. Especially if she had seen your homophobic rants on your MySpace page," I continued.

"No one uses MySpace any longer. Yes, I wrote unenlightened posts on there. But you have to understand. I am an Afghan man. I have to appear a certain way on any public forum."

"So you weren't actually opposed to your half-sister's lesbianism?" Shirley took over again.

"I admit I find the perverted lifestyle distasteful. I would not kill my cousin because of it."

"But if you had been raised in the same household you would have?"

"We weren't. And I didn't." Khalil stood and called the corrections officer to return him to his cell.

As Shirley and I returned to my car, I asked whether she believed him. As always, she reminded me it's immaterial what she believes, she collects evidence until the answers clearly point to the perpetrator, because when all other avenues have been exhausted, whatever remains, however unlikely, is the answer. Sometimes I find this frustrating. It has been my personal experience that discussing solutions, speculating, and brainstorming with my medical colleagues is not only useful, but often solves the problem. Shirley, however, is a stickler on this issue.

BACK AT THE OFFICE SHIRLEY WENT TO HER DESK TO RETURN phone calls. I went to mine and did my own brainstorming. I used mind-mapping to review details I had captured from each of the suspects. I sorted out alibis and who confirmed them, motives, and opportunities for each person on our list. When I compared Bori and Khalil now it seemed to me they were fairly equal, although I wanted to place more weight on Khalil's motives. Here was a guy, secretly hating his cousin, taking full advantage of her generosity, knowing all the time she was his rich sister who had named him in her will. (Had he known all along? This was presumption on my part. I needed to check. He hadn't denied knowing, but when did he find out?) Along comes Bori with her acid attack. All Khalil needed to do was finish off Zaro, and let Bori take the fall.

I wondered what the thinking was down at PPB. I called Shirley's contact at the bureau, told her I was asking on behalf of our investigation, and got her to tell me that both Khalil and Bori were top on Xio's list of suspects. No real help there, but at least now Shirley's contact was also mine. I felt a bit smug, if I were honest.

"Shall we go to lunch and discuss our findings?"

"Food trucks?"

"Excellent idea, doctor. We can take our lunch to the park."

"I'll bring a blanket to sit on."

We preferred to sit apart from the public when we were discussing cases. You never knew who might overhear something they shouldn't. Fortunately we were both quiet talkers and only projected loud voices when we needed to be heard. We could sit within six feet of others and not be heard by anyone other than each other. We walked over to the food trucks on NW Alder and picked up some lunch, and on to the little park between Burnside and Ash. There's a fountain, and usually a few skaters mixed in with the downtown working folks and a few homeless people. We were all seeking a bit of sun and fresh air. I put our blanket down on the grassy area several yards away from anyone else. We sat cross-legged and ate our food.

Shirley outlined what we'd discovered in the way of evidence today, and went over Khalil's interview in depth. I added what I'd seen in his face and body language. He was tense and almost confrontational during the interview, but maybe that was because he was being held for forty-eight hours by the PPB, with no real evidence to charge him with murder.

As we drank our vitamin water (in my case) and home-made ginger ale (Shirley's), I asked Shirley if she would tell me something about her family. She offered little that was new to me. She'd grown up in Kansas City, Missouri, left for Harvard and never returned to live at home. She went to school year-round to avoid going home because her parents didn't know how to be with her (her words). She said they found her too odd. I surmised she was much brighter than the rest of her family, although Mylo grew up to be an investigator as well.

"What about Mylo? You must have some things in common, what with him investigating for the KCPD."

"He's smarter than I thought he was. He's six years younger than I am, so he was only twelve when I left home. But he also attended Harvard, though it took him five years to finish, as opposed to my three."

"Did you talk about Harvard when you went home?"

"No."

"What about your cases, did you compare notes?"

"No, we took separate shifts to sit by Dad's side."

"Oh. So you must have spent a lot of time with your mother."

"No, she stayed with Dad along with Mylo."

"Shirley, I'm so sorry. For your loss of course, but also for having to bear it all alone." I wanted to say I was sorry her family were such jerks. I managed to restrain myself.

"Thank you, Mary. Any other questions?"

"Did you get to talk to your Dad, I mean was he awake and coherent for part of the time?"

"The doctors had him in an induced coma, hoping they could prolong his life with drugs and oxygen until he could rally. So, no. He died without ever waking up."

"Were you with him when he died?" I knew I was being intrusive at this point, but my curiosity got the best of me.

"No. He died while Mylo and Mom were there, but Mylo had stepped out to get coffee. So it was only Mom who was there at the end."

"You could have stayed for the funeral. I was handling the case. It helped that I knew I could call you, and that you would call for updates."

"It was time for me to leave. Everything worked out for the best, Mary. I didn't return because I didn't trust you to handle the case."

"Okay."

I'd learned everything I was going to about her trip back east. At least for the time being. We composted our food waste, recycled my bottle and her cup, and headed back to the office.

As we walked by Margolies Jewelry store, the rings caught my eye. Wouldn't a ruby make a beautiful engagement ring? Where did that idea come from? I'd only had a first date with Beth and I was already looking at rings? What the? Slow down Mary.

I should be looking at my budget, making sure I had enough surplus to not only buy the house, but to move, maybe replace some of my furniture, take care of changing the locks, securing the house, all those details.

I could call Beth and confirm she was coming over Friday evening for dinner. When she said yes, I could plan the menu. And I'd decided what I would wear.I needed to clean house, spruce up the front garden, make sure my curb appeal was up to Beth's standards.

I called Beth the minute I was back in my office with the door shut. When she said she'd be there with bells on, I headed home early to start the process of making my place comfortable, welcoming, and beautiful—for my girl.

CHAPTER SIXTEEN:
SECOND CHANCES

FRIDAY NIGHT ARRIVED IN WHAT SEEMED LIKE MINUTES. I was ready, in every way. My house was squeaky clean, the front garden mowed, trimmed, rose bushes deadheaded. I had vases of roses on several surfaces, in every room of the house. I had washed the windows, cleaned the mirrors, dipped my hanging crystals in rubbing alcohol. I'd selected a jazz compilation for the iPod and plugged it into my sound system. I lit the candles fifteen minutes before Beth was due to arrive. The salad was made, the tofu casserole was baking, the veggies were roasting, and the wine was chilling. I wore lounging pants of black silk charmeuse and a white cotton tee. Martha was groomed and her nails were clipped. I didn't want snags on my silk pants! I debated whether to go barefooted as I usually did at home, or to wear my fancy flats. Bare feet won out. I'd varnished my toenails with clear polish. My hair and body were as clean as the house. I'd put lotion on my hands because all that housework had roughened and reddened them. I had spent the last two evenings cleaning and polishing until nearly midnight. This morning I changed the sheets and fluffed the pillows. I was excited to the point of near-hysteria. So I poured myself a glass of wine and positioned myself on the chair nearest the front window. Just as I sat, Beth pulled up. I took a big gulp of the wine, put my glass on the coaster, and waited for her to approach the front door.

As I opened the door to greet Beth, my cell phone rang. It was Shirley.

"Where are you, Mary? I'm waiting by Gate Four for you."

Oh no. I had completely forgot about Oceane's concert. I was supposed to meet Shirley at the Jeld-Wen Field. We had box seats, thanks to Oceane's agent Elijah Reilly.

"Sorry, Shirley, I'm running late. I'll be right there." I hung up before she could ask me what caused the delay.

"I'm so sorry, Beth. I have to go. I totally forgot about Oceane's concert. Shirley and I are guests in a VIP box. This is work. We're on the case."

"Go, it's fine. We'll do this another time."

"Would you mind staying here long enough to take the casserole and veggies out of the oven for me? You can leave them on top of the stove, I'll deal with them when I get back. Unless you want to eat . . . Of course you do, eat, eat! There's salad in the fridge, and the wine is already cool. Help yourself. The door will lock behind you."

"I don't want to eat without you, Mary. Why don't I put everything away, and we'll have leftovers. Can you do this tomorrow night?"

"Brilliant! I can! But I have to run now." I ran all right. Into my bedroom where I quickly changed my silk pants for linen ones, and slipped on socks and shoes. Back in the living room I said, "I'll call you. Wait, just come back tomorrow night same time, can you?"

"Can and will. Now run!"

I grabbed a light jacket and ran. I sped. I used valet parking. I was there in fifteen minutes because I took side roads and shortcuts. I hurried up to Gate Four where Shirley stood like a statue.

"We have less than five minutes before the show starts. Elijah Reilly has been calling me every two seconds wanting to know where you are."

"I'm here now, let's go meet him."

Although we were outside the stadium, once inside we were mere steps away from the VIP box Reilly had arranged. There were snacks, water, and drinks of every kind available to us once we were in, all provided by the owner of the suite. But we were the only three using the space tonight. We overlooked the entire field, and had an unim-peded view of the stage. No sooner were we in our seats than the opening act began to play.

"Elijah, how is Oceane this evening?" I knew he was nervous about this big concert, and I hoped to put him at ease.

"Oceane? Oh, she's fine. She's in her element. I knew she would be, that's why I kept after her to go ahead with the concert in spite of everything."

"We appreciate your inviting us to see the concert from this box, Elijah."

"You're welcome."

"How long have you known Oceane?"

"I've been her international agent for almost a year."

Shirley chimed in with, "and how did you get the position?"

"Her business manager recommended me. He knew of my work from another group I manage."

"The one playing now?"

"No, it's a touring group called Daughters of the Opening Night. He saw them when they played in Paris, then got in touch with me."

"What do you think of Oceane?"

"She's high strung, like all artists. Like I said, I knew she'd be all right if I could get her to go ahead and perform tonight. But it was touch and go, I don't mind telling you."

"Why's that, do you think?"

"Her girlfriend, of course. Who wouldn't be upset? Then being questioned by the police and stuff. Her dad too. What a nightmare."

"But you calmed her down."

"I did. I didn't tell Oceane, of course, but she's better off without that Zaro person anyway."

"What makes you think so?"

"Are you kidding me? Zaro had her wrapped around her finger so tight, Oceane would have done anything she wanted. Including giving up her career to be a damned caretaker for the rest of her life."

His face was getting red as he warmed to the topic. We were not only shaded in the box, but it had air conditioning as well, so Elijah's increasing color had nothing to do with the environment. But Shirley did not back down.

"So even though you'd only just met Oceane, you are the one guy who was able to sooth her nerves and get her to perform?"

"That's right. That's what managers do, don't you know anything?"

"Tell me more."

"Look, she'll be coming on in a few minutes. Why don't you make yourself a drink or something? I'm going out for a smoke."

With that, he departed the box, and Shirley and I were left looking at each other. She went over to the bar, put ice in a glass and filled it with seltzer. I looked in the refrigerator, and pulled out a jug of white grape juice. I chose the largest glass, filled it halfway with club soda, then the rest of the way with juice. No ice for me. I picked up a dish filled with salted almonds, carried them to my seat, and placed them on the drinks table between me and Shirley.

As Oceane was about to come onstage, Elijah returned. He smelled like smoke, but he was chewing gum and looking dour. He clapped as Oceane entered the stage, and took his seat without looking at either of us. We joined in the applause. I was genuinely excited to see this international pop star in her entertainer persona. She looked larger, taller, more self-assured than I was used to seeing her. Her costume glittered in the lights, swished around her as she moved, and showed off her body to the utmost, without her looking bare, or as if she might have a mishap with her garment. Her voice was like velvet, silky on the upscale, soft and strong in her power range. I rarely listened to pop music, but I was enjoying this. I felt my muscles relax after about thirty seconds.

Oceane performed for more than two hours, then returned for three encores when the enthusiastic crowd simply would not stop applauding and yelling for her to come back. By the end of the concert, I was a confirmed fan determined to obtain every one of her albums and get them autographed. If I couldn't take advantage of my position as one of her team ... well, I could and I planned to do so.

All three of us were smiling and polite now. Shirley and I said goodnight to Elijah and thanked him again for the seats. I wanted to stop to buy my music, but the lines were outrageous. I decided to buy them at Powell's later. I preferred to give my business to local stores. Powell's was a bookstore, but they carried music as well. I'd get the albums the next day and get them signed before Oceane moved on to her next gig. Which, I imagined she might delay until the case was resolved, but Shirley assured me that the police would allow Oceane to continue her tour. They didn't have reason to hold her at the moment, and could easily find her if that changed. Me, I was not so sure. What would keep her from flying to a country without extradition? If she were guilty of killing Zaro, that is. I didn't believe she was. Still, had it been up to me, I would have kept everyone in Portland until the case was solved.

THE NEXT DAY WAS SATURDAY. I WAS LOOKING FORWARD TO MY evening with Beth. I hoped she truly understood about my having left her in my house on Friday night. When I returned home from the concert I found all the leftovers neatly wrapped and placed in the refrigerator. The table was still set for our dinner, but the candles had been snuffed early on. My sound system was turned off. Beth had left a lamp on in the living room for me, with a note on the table beside it. All she said was "I hope you have a great time tonight, and I'm excited to reboot our date tomorrow night! Call me."

I'd taken her at her word, and called her. She was still up, listening to KBOO's late night programming called "Plugged In." I could hear some dubstep playing in the background. It was mellow enough for me to tune out as Beth and I chatted briefly, and catchy enough that I tuned it in after we signed off. I felt as if I were floating and my face wouldn't stop smiling. I danced around my bedroom as

I turned down the bed, got out my sleep tee, and filled Martha's kibble dish on the bathroom counter. I filled her water dish too. Then it was off to bed, with the memory of Beth's laugh filling my head. I knew I would dream of her. How could I not?

The hospital room was dark, but the window was wide open and rain was blowing in. I stood at the door in my sleep tee, straining to see who it was who stood next to Zaro's bed. Whoever it was, she or he was plunging a needle into Zaro's IV line. Water rushed across the floor and hit my feet. I gasped, then slapped my hand over my mouth, too late. The person started heading my way. I turned and ran, opening the door to the stairwell, which was so dimly lit I could barely see the broken glass littering the concrete stairs. I grabbed for the rail and jumped from one landing to the next, my hand sliding effortlessly down the stair rail, my body virtually flying from one story to the next. How many stories up were we anyway? Suddenly, I was in an elevator shaft, clinging to the cables, the only sound a mewling cry like that of a baby monkey.

I awoke in a sweat, my heart racing, my throat dry. I bounded out of bed and rushed to the bathroom for a glass of water. In the glow of the nightlight I saw my tense face, and took a deep breath. It was a dream, it was only a dream. More like nightmare.

As I climbed back into bed, I glanced at the clock. Nearly four a.m. It was almost light out, and the birds were singing. I could hear the house finches calling to each other right outside my bedroom window. I needed to go back to sleep right away if I were going to be at my best later that night. I tried not to wonder what the nightmare had been about, why water, why both Zaro's murder and the memory of the Baskerville heir case. And why didn't I stand and fight Zaro's murderer, then at least I would know who we were after.

I had no answers, only a need for sleep. I put on my sleep mask, plugged my ears, gave Martha a few pets, and began meditating.

THE DAY FLEW BY. ONCE I WAS UP, THAT IS. BECAUSE OF THE earplugs, I hadn't heard my alarm. I slept until after eleven. I dashed out to do my errands, called Shirley when I came home, made sure she didn't need me. I made a foolproof dessert: mango fool. Yes, I had the cake from last night's nonstarter of a dinner, but I wanted something fresh, and who doesn't love a choice? Maybe she'd want two desserts. I put the mango fool into my smallest dessert glasses. That way, Beth could have two desserts with no guilt. Mom used to always say, "take two, they're small!" And she said it no matter what she was dishing up. Even so, she was never the kind of mom who insisted that we clean our plates, or even taste everything we'd been served. She was the kind of mother who would serve you something nineteen times before giving up, because she read somewhere that's how many times it might take someone to like a certain food.

I had a nice long soak in the tub before dinner time. I usually shower because it's quick, efficient, and doesn't use as much water. Today I wanted to be completely relaxed when Beth arrived, so a full bath with salts, a loofa, and a rinsing shower after, that was the ticket. My hair smelled like the shampoo and conditioner I'd bought for the occasion. Usually I buy something cheap that doesn't test on animals. That day at the health food market I'd bought something that smelled so heady, yet light, it could be perfume.

I chose a different outfit from last night. I wore cotton gauze pants in black with ties at the ankle, with an ultra-light ivory tee. I kept my feet bare as I had no intention of leaving the house. My floors and rugs were still clean, even the ceilings were clean. No cobwebs, no neglected corners for this date. After resetting the table with a different tablecloth, napkins, and different dishes, glasses, and silverware, I selected music for the evening and put it on. Then I put the entree and veggies in the oven to reheat, took out the salad and tossed it, and opened a new bottle of red wine to breathe.

Five minutes before Beth was due, my phone rang. When I heard Shirley's ring, I was tempted to turn off the phone. I couldn't.

"Mary?"

"Yes, Shirley?"

"I wanted to say I hope you enjoy your date tonight."

"Thanks, Shirley. I'm gonna try."

"Okay, that's all."

"All right then. Bye."

"Wait, Mary. About tomorrow."

"Yes?"

"Tomorrow is Sunday. We don't need to work tomorrow unless it's an emergency."

I smiled. I knew what it cost her to think about another person's happiness. Even mine.

"Thank you. I hope you have a good night too, Shirley."

"Of course. Goodbye then."

And she was gone. She had taken the time and effort to consider what this date might mean to me, and called me to give her blessing. With most friends it would be the normal course of events. Shirley isn't that normal. She is brilliant, she is efficient, she is productive. But she usually thinks only of her work, or sometimes of herself. In the case of her father, she thought enough of him and the rest of her family to go when called to be at his bedside until he died. She came right back to work. No sentimentality for Shirley. Her caring whether or not I had a good date tonight meant so much.

I was still smiling when I opened the door for Beth.

CHAPTER SEVENTEEN:
AFTERGLOW

Monday morning I fairly danced down the street from my car to the office. I hadn't slept more than a total of four hours since Saturday morning, but my entire body was buzzing as if I'd been injecting caffeine into my veins. My eyes felt a little gritty, but other than that I was normal. No, so much better than "normal." I wrenched my mind away from the delicious Beth Adams, and onto my work. Right, the case.

I needed to check on Khalil and the will. He hadn't denied knowing he was named, but when he found out was crucial. Knowing he was going to inherit so much money would be an enormous motive for murdering the half-sister he disapproved of. If he hadn't known, he still might have committed the murder, in spite of his saying he wouldn't carry out an honor killing in the circumstances. I got out the will, found the attorney's office phone number and called. The time difference meant it was already late afternoon there. I reached the receptionist, but the attorney was not in. I asked for his administrative assistant or secretary and was put through to a young man with a Scottish accent. His name was Craig, and he was happy to help me because I was investigating the death of their client.

"Craig, can you tell me whether Khalil knew he would come into a fortune when Zaro died?"

"I can tell you that he didn't have a copy of the will. And, of course, as an inheritor he didn't witness the will. There would not have been a reason for him to have a copy, unless Zaro herself gave it to him, or told him of her bequest."

"You've been so helpful, Craig. Thank you."

He offered to send me a list of names and addresses of people who were involved in the will, including her executor, and I happily accepted. Within minutes I had an e-mail with the information. Maybe one of these people would know who knew what when. Reminded me of what I'd read about the Reagan administration and the Iran-Contra scandal. That too was all about who knew what and when.

After all the telephone calls, most of them international, the only thing I knew was Khalil wasn't provided a copy of the will by Zaro's attorneys. I left voicemail for everyone I couldn't reach. Zaro's father was the executor for her will, but he had turned that complicated job over to his own attorney. Knowing what I knew of Zaro, I was shocked she would make her conservative father her executor. Perhaps she knew he would put those duties into the right hands. Or maybe her sense of family was stronger than I thought. It was even possible that she still loved and revered her father, having spent so many years at his side as his "son." He was cold and professional in our telephone conversation. I wondered again at Zaro's youth, spent fighting against Soviet occupation, part of the Mujahedeen.

Shirley popped her head in at lunchtime, asking me to join her. I hadn't spoken with her since her telephone call on Saturday evening. I felt a little embarrassed. Not because of anything I felt or had done, but because I knew Shirley knew. She was the only one outside of Beth and me who knew I was dating, knew I had been asexual until now, knew I was with Beth on Saturday night. She didn't know Beth and I spent from Saturday night until this morning in bed, forgoing meals, phone calls, or any other form of entertainment. I wanted to tell her, I wanted to shout it from the roof of the building. Somehow

I knew she didn't want to hear it. I'd hold my tongue unless or until she gave me a sign.

We got our meal from the food trucks, but as it was raining again, we took our lunch back to the office. As we ate at her desk, we once again went over the case. I told her what I had learned (and not learned) so far today. She told me she had gone to the Justice Center again on Sunday and re-interviewed Khalil, but he wasn't telling anything she didn't already know.

We decided to re-focus on Bori. After lunch we headed down to the Benson Hotel, Room 515. where she was staying. Bori opened the door as though she'd been standing in front of it staring out the peephole.

"What do you guys want?" She looked like she had had fifteen cups of coffee. Which is to say, bug-eyed, jumpy, and speaking too fast for her mouth. As usual.

"We're here about Zaro's murder, Bori. We want to ask you more questions." I took this one. Between Bori's nervousness, and Shirley's cold, professional tone, I was the one to try to get things started on a calm note.

"Like what?"

"May we come in? Or perhaps you'd like to come to our office?"

"Come in. I don't want to go any place."

We entered her hotel room. One of the two double beds was made, but covered with clothing, newspapers, empty snack bags and candy wrappers. A food tray from room service was on the table by the window. The two chairs were strewn with more clothes. Bori sped over to the chairs and gathered up the clothes, threw them on the bed, and gestured for us to sit. She sat on the edge of the bed near the table, crossed her legs, leaned forward and jiggled her foot.

"Well, what is it?"

"Where were you on the night Zaro was killed?" Shirley got right to the point.

"I was here. I already told you."

"The police checked with the hotel. You used your room key at 10:18 p.m., 1:07 a.m., and 2:33 a.m., and not again until much later. Where did you go between 1:07 and 2:33?"

"I went for a walk."

"In the park blocks?"

"Yes, also down through Old Town to the railroad tracks, and I walked along the tracks across the river on the Steel Bridge, and on the sidewalk by the river to the Hawthorne Bridge, crossed it and went up to Broadway and came back here."

"That is a very specific route. I'm surprised you remember it in such detail." We both knew too much detail often meant the statement was untrue.

"I should remember it, I walk there every time I go out. It takes me less than an hour in daylight, a little longer in the dark."

"You walk slower in the dark?"

"I like the quiet. It slows me down a bit."

"You aren't afraid to be out alone in the dark?"

She looked surprised. "No. Nothing has happened to me. There are some homeless people in the park blocks and under the bridges, but they haven't bothered me. I don't bother them."

"I was thinking more of the bars closing, and men who might have had too much to drink, and too little luck with women who might harass you."

"I walk far around people like that. I only want exercise, not social mixing."

"So, do you have any witnesses to this walk you took that night?"

"I spoke with the doorman on my way out."

"What about on your way in?"

"I don't remember."

"Are the police buying your story?"

"I don't understand. Why would they pay money for my story?"

"Shirley means do the police believe you?"

"They haven't arrested me, as you can see."

She had a point.

"Very well. Do you know the doorman's name?"

"No, but I'm sure the hotel could tell you." Bori jumped up from the bed as though it had bitten her. She went straight to the door, opened it and held it for us until we took the hint.

"We'll be back, Ms. Eszti. We'll speak with the doorman and get back to you."

Actually, we would also speak with the police to see if they had turned up more witnesses before getting back to Bori. The doorman who saw her leave could confirm she left, but if he didn't see her come back he couldn't say what state she was in. Of course, she was so jumpy naturally that she might not have looked any different after killing Zaro than she had before. If we didn't make headway soon, I was going to be as bug-eyed as Bori.

LATE THAT AFTERNOON I CALLED BETH. THE SWEET SOUND OF her voice calmed me and excited me at the same time. She had to show some houses that evening, so we weren't getting together. I decided to use my free time to do some laundry, vacuum, and sit down and let Martha have my full attention. We had had our first sleepover with another human. At least when the human in question was in my bed. Anyone who stayed with us before had slept on the couch. Martha took it in stride, but she hadn't got as many pettings as usual, and had even been shut out of the bedroom for hours at a time. If Martha could talk, she'd probably have questions for me. I had questions for myself, but I was in no mood to answer them. I only wanted more of the same, thank you.

Once Martha and I were ensconced in my easy chair, I had time to think. Go over the case in my mind again, replay Bori's interview with us today, and consider who could have killed Zaro. I was stuck on Bori and Khalil. But what about Oceane's father, Austin? He came into town that night, unannounced. He was an over-protective parent worried about his young daughter. He wanted her to go forward with her singing career, and he preferred she remain single, or at least out of the clutches of Zaro Sadozai. His feelings about Zaro were intense and well-known. He was staying at the Benson too. Did he have in and out times in the middle of that night? I'd follow that up. If he were the killer, how did he get into the VIP ward? He wasn't familiar with Portland, didn't have a car. Would he have taken the number eight bus up to the hill? Maybe a taxi. Either would be risky in the middle of the night as passengers were more likely to be remembered. Who would have let him in? Oceane had gone "home" to the yacht. Austin didn't know anyone else in Portland. Did he? I'd follow that up as well.

Maybe I should focus on motives for each suspect. Austin, we knew. He wanted to "save" his daughter. Bori was seeking revenge, though she claimed she was satisfied having shot Zaro with acid. Khalil would have to be either honor killing or for the money. Elijah Reilly was a slob, but he hadn't even known Zaro. His motive? Keeping Oceane on track, the same as Austin's, really.

It seemed to me we needed to focus on opportunity. But I was stuck. I couldn't imagine anyone having the opportunity unless it was someone who worked at the hospital. Why would any of the nurses or doctors or other hospital workers have reason to kill Zaro?

Yet Zaro was dead, and someone had killed her. It wasn't an accident. A person, probably a person I'd met and talked with this week, had deliberately injected an overdose of morphine into Zaro's IV line. When I tried to put a face on the killer in this scenario, it was Bori who flashed like a blinking light in my mind. That only sent me back to how? How did she get in, get past the security of the VIP ward?

And that sent me to sleep.

I awoke when a pain in my neck pinched hard enough to make me sit up. I had fallen into a slump, leaning sideways in my chair, drooling on my shirt. The house was dark, Martha was long gone, and when I tried to stand up, my leg was asleep. I nearly went over, but managed to catch myself and sit down again. I stomped my foot, rubbed my calf, and kept blinking until my leg and I were awake enough to try again. This time I made it to the kitchen, turned on a light and found Martha snoozing on the counter. No wonder I found cat hair in my food sometimes, the little sneak. I was going to have to remember to wipe down the counters every single time I used them.

After a light supper, I showered and went to bed. For real this time. Martha joined me there. I fell asleep to the sound of her purring.

At breakfast the next morning I felt certain that I knew the answer to how to solve this murder, but I couldn't quite bring it to the front of my brain. Maybe Shirley knew by now. She was always ahead of me, and with me feeling so close, she was probably simply tying up loose ends. I hurried through my time at home, and went to the office.

SHIRLEY WAS GONE. SHE CAME IN EARLY, GATHERED UP SOME files, and left without telling Lix where she was headed. I wanted to call her cell right away and find out where her thinking was. I didn't. If she wanted me to be with her, she'd have asked. On the other hand, I didn't want to pursue some thread on the case without checking in to see whether she'd already covered it. I stewed about this over coffee for an hour. Finally, I took my cell out of my pocket to call her, and it cried "Help!" in my hand.

"Shirley!"

"I'm at OHSU. I need you to come pick me up right away. I took the bus up here, but we need to drive."

"I'll be right there. Where will you be waiting?"

"At the bus stop on Sam Jackson Road across from the children's hospital."

"See you in fifteen."

I couldn't wait to find out where we were headed, but I hadn't asked because I knew Shirley didn't want to take the time on the phone. It's not her way. I grabbed two full water bottles on my way out. We keep our own stainless steel water bottles full and ready to go, both at home and in the office. We had some made up with the name of our company on them: Combs and Watson, Private Investigations, Inc. I wanted to hand them out to all and sundry, but Shirley would only give them to our actual clients. What could have been a great marketing tool, in my opinion, was merely swag. Naturally, I had half a dozen of them myself. The two I brought fit into my car's cup holders. I tossed my bag into the back, and made it up to the hill in twelve minutes. Shirley was right where she said she'd be. I made a u-turn in the hospital drive and picked her up at the bus stop.

"Go as quickly as you can to Elijah's apartment."

Luckily, I never let my gas tank drop below half. In this business, you always have to be ready to travel. From OHSU to Elijah's apartment was about thirteen miles by highway. At this time of day, we should make it in twenty-five minutes or less.

"What do you have?"

"I've learned how a person could get into the VIP ward without signing in. I've also learned that Elijah Reilly's mother was in the hospital at the same time as Zaro. Not in the VIP ward, of course, but in the same building. We need to interview him again."

"Elijah? Do you seriously think he killed Zaro?"

"I don't speculate, you know that."

"Yes, but, do you think he might have?"

"Anyone might have. You might have. You know how to get into the ward, you know how to kill someone with morphine, you might have wanted to put us into the national spotlight by performing this as a publicity stunt."

I nearly ran off the road.

"What? That's outrageous! I would never kill anyone."

"Any human being is capable of killing."

"Don't be so literal. Being capable isn't the same thing as actually taking a human life. I'm a doctor! I've sworn the Hippocratic Oath, which specifies that 'I will give no deadly medicine to anyone if asked, nor suggest any such counsel' among other things. I'm in the business of saving lives, not killing people."

"Mary, please. I'm making a point. Calm down before you become reckless in your driving."

She had a point. My mind was not on the highway. I nearly missed the exit to I-84E. I pulled myself back to reality by focusing on my breath, my body, my hands on the wheel.

"Sorry. If we are merely discussing possibilities, you could put yourself in the same scenario you stuck me."

"True. And now that you've made that point, please apply it to Elijah. The fact is, if he could get in, why not Bori, Khalil, Austin?"

"You said Elijah's mother was in the hospital the same time as Zaro though."

"Which is why we need to talk with him."

"Right."

We sat in silence the rest of the way. Shirley no doubt knew what she would ask Elijah. I wanted to accuse him. Once again, I was reminded of how much I had to learn from Shirley. Her coolly intellectual mind would never be mine, but I could practice cooling down, practice holding onto my thoughts without letting them turn into suppositions, or worse: accusations.

As we pulled into the parking lot, Elijah was leaving his apartment.

CHAPTER EIGHTEEN:
A COMMON LOON

I HATED BEING WRONG. OF COURSE I'D RATHER BE HAPPY than right, but I was pretty unhappy when proved wrong. Case in point: out in the East, people frequently are treated to the cry of the common loon when they are around water, particularly wooded lakes. It's one of the things I always looked forward to during vacation. My family would go to a cabin on a lake in Maine for a week or two every year. At night, and again in the early morning, we'd hear the lonely sound of the loons calling to each other. When I moved to Portland, it became one of the things I missed from "back home." Every time I saw a movie or television show purportedly set in the Pacific Northwest and they put in a loon's song, I was aggravated. The sound pulled me out of my suspended belief and made me wish "they'd get it right."

On the way to Elijah's apartment, we passed near a reservoir. Shirley said, "Oh look, Mary, a common loon." I nearly drove into the lane divider.

"There aren't any loons on the west coast. You must be mistaken."

"No, Mary, common loons live all over the continent. They winter along the coast and are found near lakes, reservoirs, even on the Willamette and Columbia Rivers. This pair must have come in early. Although they could live here year-round. It's not unheard of."

Shut my mouth. I knew Shirley wouldn't make up this information. But I was so dazed by it, I missed our exit off I-84, and had to drive several miles out of the way because of it. Shirley sat in silence, no doubt trying to make the car go faster with her mind.

By the time we reached Elijah's, he was coming out his front door. I braked in front of him. Shirley quickly opened the passenger-side door and placed herself in his path. I turned off the ignition and followed suit. I would park the car, once we were allowed in to speak with him.

He was having none of it. "Get out of my way, both of you. I don't have time for your bullshit."

"We simply want to ask you a few more questions, Mr. Reilly."

"Well, Ms. Combs, I don't want to answer them. Now get out of my way, or I'll shove you out of my way."

As he raised his arms to give her a shove, Shirley grabbed his arm, stepped into his body, and slammed him into my car. He slid to the ground, jumped up and tried again. This time she threw him to the ground and stepped on his outflung arm.

"Okay okay, you made your point. Come inside. I don't want my neighbors watching a hundred pound girl beat me up."

"I am not a girl, I'm a woman. And my weight is one hundred thirty pounds. Clearly you've been misinformed about how much a slender 'girl' can weigh."

"Whatever."

"Shirley, I'll park the car and be right in."

She nodded and they went inside. I was inside within two minutes. They were seated opposite each other, Shirley on the edge of her chair, Elijah plopped down on the couch on top and in the midst of what looked like a month's worth of dirty clothes. The usual food detritus continued to cover every flat surface.

"You were saying, about your mother?"

"Yeah, she's been in the hospital. What of it?"

"Which hospital, for what, and from when to when, if you don't mind, Mr. Reilly."

"OHSU, and she's got bone cancer. She's dying, all right?"

"When did she enter the hospital, and when did she go home?"

"She went in around the middle of May. She's still there. Satisfied?"

"Why do you live like this, Mr. Reilly? You manage international stars. Your commission has to be at least ten to fifteen percent."

"Health care is expensive."

"Yes, it is. But I've spoken with the billing department at OHSU, and it seems your mother's bills are all paid by Medicaid. Not by her son."

"Medicaid only goes so far. They're gonna discharge her eventually and she'll need hospice care."

"Medicaid in Oregon covers hospice care, one hundred percent."

"How I spend my money is none of your business."

We were getting somewhere. Finally.

"I'm afraid it very much is our business. We are investigating the murder of the fiancée of your client. You are one of the suspects in this murder."

"But I have an alibi."

"And that is?"

"I was out of town."

"Out of town where?"

"Seattle. My clients 'Morning Glory Hole' were opening for Sound Garden that night. I stayed overnight. Didn't get back here until late afternoon."

"And you have people who can vouch for you?"

"Sure. The band and I stayed at one of their friend's houses in Kirkland. We partied all night. Must have been a hundred people there."

"Give me a list of names and telephone numbers. We'll check your alibi and get back to you."

"Screw you. I already did that with the police. They confirmed it already. Check with them."

"We'd like to make these calls ourselves. So please give me a list."

"I'm leaving."

Shirley sighed. "Please don't make me have to hold you down so you can give us the names. But if I have to, let's go outdoors. I prefer fresh air when I exercise."

"Fine. I don't have any paper."

"I have some," I said as I offered both paper and pen.

Elijah got out his phone, wrote down ten names (so much for the hundred witnesses), thrust the list back at me—not Shirley—and headed for the door. He held it open until we were both clear, and slammed it so hard I knew his hinges must have loosened. He rushed off to the Max stop, and Shirley didn't offer him a ride downtown.

When I went to get the car from its spot, I walked around the car, checking for damage from the two combatants. Some of the dirt had been smeared, but Elijah's body hadn't marked it otherwise.

BACK IN THE OFFICE, SHIRLEY AND I DIVIDED UP THE LIST OF names and began calling. As always, we got mostly voicemail. Rarely did I ever get a busy signal these days. That would have to come from a land line, which most people rarely used. There was the fact that hardly anyone answered an unscreened call, and even if these people saw our names on their screens, they weren't likely to recognize us. I made a note of this point for my next pitch for marketing. Our calls might be answered more readily if the answerers' screens told them we were calling from Combs and Watson, Private Investigations, Inc. once they were familiar with the name. A few late night television spots, more articles in the free weeklies, appearances on the local talk shows. Either of us could do those. Word of mouth isn't everything. Personally, I'd like it if we got a few easy cases, like missing property rather than murder. Of course, this one hadn't started out as a murder case. I don't know how easy it would have been to get Oceane to see Zaro as the lying, murderous woman she was, but it would have been educational to find out whether we could do it. We hadn't had a missing jewel case since the Pittock Mansion one. The PPB didn't have the resources to track down stolen cars. I thought that would be easier than solving murders. Why didn't people hire us for that? Because we didn't advertise. Another point for my pitch.

I'd been daydreaming as I dialed the numbers. Finally an answer came when I wasn't ready. I had my mouth full of water.

"Hello? Hello? Who's calling me? I can see your number here, so forget about doing heavy breathing..."

"I'm sorry, hello. This is Dr. Mary Watson with Combs and Watson, Private Investigations. I'm calling to confirm something with you."

"I'm not buying anything."

"No, no, I'm not selling. You're a friend of Elijah Reilly, right?"

"I know Elijah."

"Have you seen him lately?"

"Why? Is he missing?"

"No, let me rephrase. When did you last spend time with Elijah?"

"I saw him at a party not long ago. We hung out a little there."

"When was that?"

He gave me the date of the night before Zaro was murdered in the early morning.

"What time did he leave? Do you remember?"

"He was still there when I left at five in the morning."

"Do you know what time he got there?"

"Nah. He was there when I got there though."

"What time was that?"

"I'm not sure. It was after the bars closed. So maybe two-thirty or three?"

"And he was already there."

"Yep, and pretty buzzed."

"Do you remember who else was there when you got there that night?"

He named four people already on our list.

"Thank you, Mr. Kirby. I appreciate your help."

"Yeah, whatever."

Lovely people Elijah hung out with.

I checked in with Shirley to let her know my results so far. I also let her know that two of the people on her half of the list had been at the party with Elijah at two-thirty or three the morning of the murder. Or so said Jeff Kirby. She had spoken with Chester Sheldon. He was a temp nurse who had worked at OHSU the week before the murder. He met Elijah there when Chester was caring for Elijah's mom. They had gone to the party together. According to Chester, they'd arrived at the party before midnight and had stayed until after five.

Now we waited to hear back from everyone with whom we'd left a message.

Meanwhile, Shirley went back over every detail of the case, adding notes to the timeline, notes to each person's individual file, and placing blank Post-Its under each person's photo that she had up on her murder board. Before I could ask about the blanks, Shirley wrote a question on one under Elijah's picture. "Did he have an accomplice?"

My question would have been more along the lines of "what would he gain from killing Zaro?" Aside from keeping Oceane as a client, I couldn't see it. Anyway, Oceane might have continued her career once she'd had a chance to either honeymoon with Zaro, or have had the scales lifted from eyes and have seen who the real Zaro was. Even with Zaro temporarily needing Oceane's care, she wouldn't have become dependent on Oceane in the long run. Zaro might have dumped Oceane for being too clingy once she was up and around. In any case, Elijah could get more clients, he got Oceane and she would have given him references. Losing her wasn't a strong enough motive for him to murder Zaro. He had no police record, no reputation for violence. The only thing we had turned up on Elijah was his stint in rehab. He had a drug problem, and obviously still did. Many people have to attend rehab more than once before they can give up their addictions.

I took a coffee break and called Beth. She was working where I'd first met her at Healthcare Supply. The receptionist put me through to her line. She was busy showing a client around and said she'd return my call as soon as she could.

I was still waiting to hear back from the partiers, so I got out paper and pen and tried to write a poem for Beth. I hadn't written a poem since I was an undergrad. My struggles turned into doodles. Hearts mostly. What next? Was I going to start writing Mrs. and Mrs. Beth Adams or Dr. and Mrs. Watson on my notebook? I wadded up my paper and tossed it into the recycle bin. I wrote pages of notes about the case. I thought maybe if I compared my notes to Shirley's, something new might turn up.

Throughout the afternoon we received returned calls from Elijah's party-going friends. One by one they each said they didn't remember what time Elijah got there, or what time he left. Everyone agreed he was there at some point for some length of time. No one saw anything unusual. As in he wasn't acting strange.

I called Beth and reached her this time. I asked if she'd join me for dinner. She suggested I come to her house and she'd pick up takeout on the way home. I said I'd be there at seven, and I left to go spend time with kitty Martha before I headed out to Beth's. I sort of expected Beth would invite me to stay the night once I was there. I packed an overnight bag and stowed it in the trunk of my car. If she asked, I'd be ready. If she didn't, no harm done. I wondered whether I was supposed to be the one to suggest our spending the night together, and remembered all the advice that told me to be myself. It would be another evening of wait and see. But first I petted, brushed, and fed Martha, cleaned her cat box, and put out fresh water. I petted her some more before showering and changing into casual clothes. I grabbed a bottle of wine from the rack and drove to the southeast side of Portland. It was a glorious evening. The sun was setting among clouds streaked with orange, purple, gold and violet. The river was calm and dragon boats were under the Sellwood Bridge as I crossed it. The temperature was in the low sixties, but warm enough for me to drive with windows down. My heart overflowed with feeling for my new love. Her smiling face seemed to loom in front of my windshield as I made my way toward her and her loving arms.

"You made it." Beth was practically purring as she pulled me inside her foyer.

"Barely. I couldn't see the road for imagining your smile."

"Get in here."

We fell into each other's arms as if we hadn't seen one another for weeks. Within minutes we were unclothed and in her bed. This time I was ready and a tiny bit more experienced. Rather than wonder what would happen next, I shivered in anticipation at every move I was about to make, and in delight at every move of Beth's.

Three hours later we sat in her kitchen in the buff, noshing on the now cold takeout, drinking the wine I brought. As we clinked our glasses in a toast to ourselves, my phone cried "Help!" and I ran to get it from my pocket.

"Mary, there's been another murder. Meet me at Colonel Summers Park on the Taylor side by the picnic pavilion."

"I'll be there in ten minutes."

I slipped into my clothes, kissed my girl goodbye, and made the short drive to Colonel Summers Park. There were police cars lined up on Taylor from 17th to 20th Avenue. I found a small spot for my car on the cross street and walked over, dreading what I was about to see.

CHAPTER NINETEEN:
DOWN AND OUT

C olonel Summers Park was one of Portland's smaller parks, but had a great attraction for neighborhood people. For one thing, it had a community garden on one corner. For another, the outer side street was Belmont with easy access to the bus line. There was the pavilion where events were held and where teens gathered late at night, some with their skateboards, some with drugs, and some just to hang out. Tonight the pavilion held a murder victim, about fifteen or twenty police, and Shirley Combs. I joined her when I spotted her mass of hair above the sea of uniforms. She was talking with one of Lt. Xio's detectives, Lydia Stolowitz. Lydia was opposite Shirley in so many ways. She was shorter by about eight inches, wider by about four sizes, and had her hair pulled back so tight in a low ponytail that she looked nearly bald. Her pale skin was a match for most Portlanders, however. There weren't many women in Person Crimes, and even fewer women of color.

"What's going on?" I asked.

"It looks as though Chester Sheldon was killed and dumped here." Shirley filled me in.

"We haven't formally identified the victim," said Stolowitz.

"I recognized him, but they'd already found his identification tag in his pocket before I came over. I heard it on the police scanner," said Shirley.

"How did he die?"

"It looks like there was a fight, but they don't know yet how he died."

"We won't know until the M.E. gives us a report," clarified Stolowitz.

Shirley pulled me away from the pavilion where we could talk without being corrected by the PPB. We sat on a picnic table about twenty yards from the action. As we were still within the crime scene tape which had sprung up around us, we weren't going to be over-heard by the public, who were growing in number.

"Shirley, what do you think killed Chester?" I knew better than to ask her who.

"It could be many different things. But they know Chester was killed somewhere else and dumped here, due to the lividity. Also, there's no sign of struggle anywhere near the body."

"He's the nurse who looked after Elijah's mom. Plus he went to that party with Elijah. I'll bet it's drugs."

"You may be correct, Mary. But it could also have been a heart attack. Or maybe he was strangled, or asphyxiated. He could have a broken neck."

"He didn't have any marks on his neck, and it didn't look broken to me."

"There are too many unknowns at this point to speculate."

"But?"

"I think we might go have a chat with Elijah."

"Let's go. Want me to drive?"

"Please."

We didn't tell Stolowitz we were leaving, not that she would care. We hopped into my car and headed out to Elijah's. I didn't know about Shirley, but I didn't expect to find anything there except Elijah himself. Shirley tried calling him on the way, but he didn't pick up.

No lights were on at Elijah's apartment. We rang and knocked without result. We whipped out our powerful flashlights and examined the area for signs of struggle. We looked for footprints in the mud, from the puddles on the walk to the door, on the concrete steps. We examined the door for any sign of a break-in. I moved to the parking lot by following footprints from Elijah's stoop. They were not perfectly formed, so it took a bit of doing, but I found a spot where he had climbed into a car. Not the car that currently inhabited the spot unless he leaped into the car from three feet away from its door. Indeed, the parked car's hood was still warm. Did that mean Elijah had left recently? I got down on the ground and shone my light under the car. The concrete was thoroughly wet. This spot had been empty for some time before the recent addition. I searched a bit more before I reported back to Shirley.

"Looks like he left more than an hour ago. And based on his footprints, he was either a passenger in someone else's car, or he had backed his car into the parking spot. He got directly into the car without going to the trunk first, and he wasn't carrying anything heavy."

"Good job, Mary. I don't see anything here to indicate the murder took place at this apartment complex. We don't know that Elijah and Chester were together, but if they were, it wasn't here. Let's go."

"Where to?"

"Let's go to the office. I want to pace, and I'd like a cup of coffee."

The rain started up again after we'd gone about half a mile. Not much more than a drizzle, but enough for the wipers. It was nearly midnight, but clearly we were going to be up for awhile. I drove through an all-night coffee spot on Burnside as we headed into the city. One thing I loved about Portland was being able to get good coffee any time I wanted it. Some people were loyal to a specific roaster, but I found there were several good ones, and spread my love around.

At the office there was no one else in the building. Weeknights would be a different story, but we were the only ones burning the midnight oil that night. We turned on every light in the place. We went to our separate offices to work. Shirley paced in order to think. I thought I would see what news I could learn from the internet, and from the police bureau. I called the bureau first, chatted up the detective who answered Lydia Stolowitz's line, and learned nothing.

Online I read breaking news for anything I could find about Chester or his murder. He hadn't been officially identified yet, nor was there news of where the killing happened. I decided to take a different tack.

I researched Elijah's mother. Erin Reilly had a FaceBook page. I read her entire timeline, beginning in 2008 when she created her page. Erin posted regularly and had more than a hundred friends. She sometimes posted photos of Elijah and his band, Elijah and her together, and Elijah and his friends. Back then he had been almost plump. He obviously had lived on fast food and beer. There were backstage pictures of him and his band smoking what appeared to be marijuana. Erin always posted about how much she loved him, and sometimes she talked about how worried she was about him. She didn't like him touring because she worried about his diet and his safety traveling late at night on unfamiliar roads.

Late last year she began posting about her health issues and calling for prayers, good vibes, and thoughts. Her friends responded daily with concern. As time went on, she began to seem less hopeful for herself. Elijah went into rehab for his addiction to cocaine and alcohol. During his month in the center, Erin seemed relieved but her own health was rapidly deteriorating. Two months ago, Elijah was released. He was excited about working with Oceane, and Erin hinted at possible new clients with big names. She was grateful for the money that Elijah was pouring into her treatment. An experimental treatment might prolong her life. She was going to enter OHSU to obtain the treatment, but Medicaid wouldn't cover the cost of the drug itself or anything experimental. She needed thousands of dollars a day to pay for it. Friends suggested she try crowd sourcing, but she assured everyone that Elijah was handling it.

"Shirley, I found something I think you should see." She came into my office, her hair bushed out around her face where she'd been running her hands through it, as she sometimes does when she's thinking hard.

"What is it?"

"It might be a motive. See what you think." I pointed her to Erin's posts beginning with her statement regarding the costs of the experimental treatment and ending with Elijah's being able to handle it.

"I agree, Mary. Now run the financials on him and let's see how well Elijah was handling those costs."

Neither of us was surprised to see that Elijah's expenditures far outstripped his income. Every credit card was maxed out. His savings were depleted, and his checking account contained barely enough to see him through the week.

"He was desperate to keep Oceane working."

"I agree, Mary. He may have been desperate enough to kill Zaro."

"But what does Chester have to do with it?"

"Chester could have provided him access to the VIP suite."

"Oh. Right. And Chester would have known how to program the Carescape B850."

"He would also have been a witness to Zaro's murder."

"And now he's dead."

"We need to find the site of Chester's murder. Not that the police aren't looking for it as well, but we might be better equipped to suss it out."

"You mean you might. I don't have a clue."

"We know it wasn't Elijah's. We need to determine where Elijah and Chester met, and where Elijah is now."

Easier said than done. How were we going to figure out where they met? Or where Elijah had gone tonight? As Shirley went back to pacing, I decided to step outside and go for a walk. I locked the doors behind me, and turned toward the river. There would be others on the waterfront walking or running or even biking in the dark, so I felt safe. The rain had stopped, and the air was cool. I turned up the collar on my jacket, shoved my hands in my pockets, and picked up the pace.

I stopped for the walk light at the next corner. I felt a sharp pain in my head, saw flashing lights, and fell down and out. The attack happened so fast I hadn't heard a thing.

When I came around and tried to open my eyes, I realized I was blindfolded. My hands were tied behind my back. Even my legs were bound at the ankle. I was lying on the hard metal floor of a van, and we were moving fast. I thought we must be on the freeway, so I listened. Hard. Yes, other vehicles also moving fast. No braking. Not much turning of the steering wheel. I rolled to my other side, as quietly as I could. I didn't want my abductor to know I was awake yet. My cell phone was in my back pocket, still there. I wriggled my hands up to reach my pocket. For this I had to roll a bit more. I was almost on my face. I inched the phone out until I had a firm grasp on it, and rolled back so if someone saw me they wouldn't see my hands, already at work, trying to call Shirley. I knew if I could get her, she'd call 911 and tell them I was in trouble. Hopefully, they'd use the GPS of my phone to find me before the van driver reached our destination and killed me.

With no speed dial on my iPhone, I had to push the home button, slide the lock, push the phone app on the bottom left, and call Shirley from my list of favorites. Hers was the top number. I hope I'd got it when I kept pushing what I saw in my mind as the right places to make my phone reach her. I couldn't find the mute button, but pushed the volume level as low as it would go. I was so focused on this task I didn't notice right away that the driver was slowing. And making a stop before turning right and continuing on, but at only about 30mph. I hoped he wasn't taking me so far away so the cavalry wouldn't find me before he stopped.

Meanwhile, I sent out telepathic messages to Shirley to find me, and hurry. I prayed I had pushed Shirley's info on my phone, and not my second favorite, which was my parents' house in Connecticut where it was the middle of the night. They would either let it go to voicemail, or they'd be frantic with worry. If they were panicking, would they call Shirley? Please let it be yes. I swore the next time I talked with them I would tell them to always call Shirley if they couldn't reach me.

The van rattled on, twisting, turning, going uphill and down, with few stops. Every time the driver slowed down for a stop, my heart raced, and I could feel the adrenaline gearing up inside me. These were obviously stop signs, as we moved forward right away and the engine was never turned off. I had tried to count the left and right turns, but got lost after the second turn. I had no idea where we were. It all depended on which freeway the driver took from downtown. And I had been unconscious, probably for only a few minutes—enough to get me bound and into the vehicle— but I couldn't be sure. With the blindfold on, I didn't even know whether it was still night. I presumed it was because I felt as though I'd been out only a short while. But how did one feel when she'd been knocked out for a few hours? I didn't have experience with this. If we had been on I-5 going south, we might be somewhere in southwestern Oregon. If we'd headed into Washington, we must be headed east. West, we'd be on the coast by now, or still on our way. East, we'd be in the Columbia Gorge. I simply couldn't tell which direction we were going. I was pretty certain the driver was alone. I could hear only one person. If there were two, wouldn't they be talking? Wouldn't one of them be keeping an eye on me?

Besides, when I thought about it, there was only one person I could think of who would have abducted me. Chester Sheldon's killer. I was working on only one case. This guy had killed Chester, and I was convinced by now that he had also killed Zaro. Now he was fighting for his life, trying to keep from being discovered. Chester must have been his accomplice at the hospital. Did he threaten to expose the murderer? What else could have triggered the necessary rage to kill him? I could be wrong, of course. Maybe Chester was a victim of assault and robbery at the park, and got killed in the process. If he was there selling or buying drugs, it could have gone wrong. But if that were the case, who abducted me?

Maybe it was a case of mistaken identity. Or maybe it was a serial killer and I happened to be in the wrong place at the wrong time.

The adrenaline was causing my mind to race and consider wild possibilities. Seriously, this had to be Elijah in the driver's seat. I considered calling out to him, as he had not taped my mouth. Given that, he must be waiting for me to speak. So I changed my mind and stayed silent, mimicking deep sleep as best I could.

After what seemed like hours, the van pulled off the road to the left, drove slowly for a short while, and parked. My mouth was so dry, I couldn't have spit if my life depended on it. I swallowed as best I could when the driver was outside the van and before he opened up the back doors. At that point, I thought I would faint from fear, but somehow forced myself to channel that fear into strength. My muscles felt as if they were expanding, and I felt my feet inside my shoes, happy I was wearing my sensible oxfords with my jeans.

The chill night air flooded the van as the driver grabbed my ankles and pulled me to the ground as if I were a sack of flour. When my feet touched the pavement, I stood up rather than fall to the ground. He was so close I could smell his breath and nervous sweat. With hands and ankles bound I didn't have much to fight with. But I used my head. Literally. I butted him in the chin with everything I had. He fell back and swore, but he didn't go down. Now he grabbed me by the elbow and pulled me forward. I had to hop or be dragged. I chose dragging. It would slow him down. I fell backward, pulling him downward. He lost control of my arms for a second, and turned me around so he could get hold of my ankles and began dragging me. Frankly, this hurt like hell. My wrists were bound behind my back and he was dragging me on my back. I tucked my hands down the waistband of my jeans rather than have my bones broken, but now I was getting knocked on the back of the head constantly.

Fortunately, he didn't have far to go. He pulled me up into a standing position, got behind me, pushed me forward in hopping steps, stopped me and pulled off my blindfold. I screamed. Yes, I screamed like a girl. I was standing on the precipice of a cliff overlooking the Columbia River. Directly below were railroad tracks, and on the other side of them, I-84, and the river on the far side. The drop-off was lined with bushes, briars, and trees. There was an enormous evergreen to my right about six feet below. It was dark out, overcast but not raining, and I knew exactly where we were. He was parked in the lower area of the lot of Portland Women's Forum state scenic viewpoint, a small park in which to enjoy the landscape below. All he had to do was push me forward and I was dead. If only we were closer to that tree, but he knew what he was up to.

"Elijah, what are you doing? Why did you bring me here?"

"Shut up."

"If you're going to kill me, I have the right to know why at least."

"You and that nosy bitch Combs. You've ruined my life."

"What? How did we do that?"

"You never stop. Never leave a person alone. Coming to my apartment, calling my friends. I tried to warn you."

"How? How did you warn me?" I made this personal.

"I called your office. I left a message."

"But I didn't get it, Elijah. I would have left you alone if I'd received the message."

"Liar! You and Combs. Liars. Lying bitches. All I needed was for Oceane to come back to work so I could keep getting paid."

"You were helping your mom, right?"

"That's right. But I can't help her unless I make a lot of money, and that means Oceane. You two messed that up."

"No, see, we were on the same side, Elijah. We were trying to get Oceane to leave Zaro. That's why we were hired." In the distance I thought I heard sirens. Please let them be coming for me.

"Bullshit. You were never on my side. You were always coming around, turning up your noses at my life."

"I swear we were hired by Oceane's father to get her away from Zaro." The sirens screamed by on the highway below. Two cop cars. I couldn't tell if they were sheriffs, state police, or what. It didn't matter, they were gone.

"What about after Zaro was dead? Your job was finished. Why didn't you lay off?"

"Oceane hired us to find Zaro's killer. We haven't succeeded yet." I heard a car shut off its engine somewhere nearby.

I teetered as my energy seemed to ebb and flow. I was listening as hard as I could for any sign of rescue. Elijah was focused solely on me. I considered falling back into him, but was afraid he'd react by pushing me forward and I'd go over the edge. A strong breeze kicked up and blew the sweat on my face dry. I began to shiver. The temperature during the day had been in the low seventies, but at night it dropped to the high forties. Even with a light jacket, I was cold, although the shivers could have been from the adrenaline.

Elijah jerked back on my arm, and let go as he was pulled backwards with an arm around his throat. During his struggle, he kicked me forward and I fell over. This time I didn't scream, just yelled something nonverbal as I tumbled over and over down the side of the mountain. I crashed through blackberry bushes, then I was sliding, and rolling head over heels. This was the end. I thought about my parents back on the east coast whom I hadn't seen in a year. I thought about Beth and wondered if she'd remember me. I thought about kitty Martha and who would take care of her.

There were no trees to stop me before I bounced when I hit a ledge. I think the bushes slowed my progress a bit. Fortunately I stopped. When I scooted my body so I could look up the mountain instead of down onto the railroad tracks, I realized how close I had come to dying. I was shaken to the core. Everything hurt, but I was dazed. I wanted to freeze in place and maybe cry for a few hours. Instead, I tried to get my wrists apart.

I could feel a piece of tape dangling from my wrist now, so I grabbed it and pulled. Apparently all the scraping during my fall had worked the tape loose. I put my mind completely on freeing my hands until I managed to pull my left one out of its bondage. Now that my hands were loose, I sat up and freed my ankles.

I looked up the mountain and saw no one. From my vantage point, I could hear nothing but the highway below and the wind blowing. I glanced over my shoulder, trying to gauge how much room I had on this ledge. I was afraid to stand up in case I went over the side. I got onto my knees and felt the side of the mountain with both hands, looking for leverage. I was getting nowhere fast.

"Mary! Mary are you down there? Can you hear me?"

"Shirley! I'm here. About halfway down, on a ledge."

"Don't move. I'll get some rope and haul you up."

"No! Don't leave me, Shirley." And the floodgates opened. I cried. I sobbed. I wanted my mommy. But I was alone. Shirley headed for rope without waiting for my pitiful reply. At least she didn't hear me boo-hooing like a baby. I wiped my face with my jacket sleeve, took a deep breath, and committed to doing whatever it took to get out of this predicament. I had a vision of something I saw on youtube called "The Perils of Pauline." A literal cliff hanger, that was me. I started laughing hysterically and couldn't stop.

Sirens approached, raced into the little park, and stopped. The lights were swirling red and blue above me. It was another minute or so before the rope came flying at me, a weight attached to the end to help her aim. I saw Shirley with an LED headlamp on peering over the edge.

"Tie this around your waist, and hold on tight and walk yourself up the cliff, Mary!"

"You can't hold me!"

"It's not only me, Mary. The deputies are helping." I saw the outlines of two heads with uniform caps on, on either side of Shirley. My right ankle wouldn't support my weight, but I hopped on the other leg for all I was worth. In no time I was up and safe.

CHAPTER TWENTY:
WRAP PARTY

E LIJAH WAS TAKEN INTO CUSTODY, AND BROUGHT TO THE
Justice Center. He confessed to the murders of both Zaro and
Chester, as well as to kidnapping me. They decided not to charge
him with attempted murder in my case. By confessing he avoided
the death penalty.

As we thought, Chester Sheldon had been Elijah's accomplice
in the murder of Zaro. According to Elijah, Chester got him into
the VIP ward, turned off the machines, and Elijah administered the
morphine. He had convinced Chester to go on a ride with him to
the coast, but Elijah had pulled off onto a logging road so they could
get high. Once stopped, Elijah hit him in the head with a brick, and
when Chester was out, he injected him with a lethal dose of morphine. All this fit in with the M.E.'s findings. Elijah followed Shirley
and me from Colonel Summers Park to his apartment, and to our
offices, where he waited outside hoping for a break. He wanted to
kill both of us, but I was the one who went out for a walk. He hit
me with the same brick he'd used on Chester, as it was still in the van.
Fortunately for me, he'd used up the last of the morphine on Chester,
so he had to find another way to kill me.

Shirley called the police as soon as she got my call from the van
and used the coordinates from my phone to find me. Because I was

out of the Portland Police jurisdiction, they had to call the local sheriff to get me. They sent out two cars and deputies to find me, but Shirley got there first.

"Next time you go out for a walk at night, Mary, remember to pay attention to your surroundings."

"I won't be walking anywhere soon, with this broken ankle." It was true, my ankle was broken, my body was bruised from head to foot, I was covered in road rash, and I'd suffered a mild concussion. The hospital emergency room fixed me up pretty quick. And I had a prescription for enough pain killers to keep me indoors for a week.

"Oh, that's a walking cast. You'll be up and around in a day."

"I can't drive though."

"So you're not planning to come to the office until you're out of the cast?"

"That's right. I'm going to stay home. In a week or so, you can send me work to do on my computer."

"Lix can do anything that needs doing on the computer, Mary. I need you."

"You can come to me. Or pick me up and bring me to work."

"We'll hire a car and driver for you until you can drive again."

"I can't afford that!" I didn't want to pay for it, whether I could afford to or not. I had the house I was closing on. I had furniture to buy. Most pressingly, I had a new girlfriend I wanted to be with.

"The business can afford it and it will be tax deductible. You are a 'key man' of the organization, and I need you at work. A day or two at home and you'll be fine."

"The business can afford to hire a driver?"

"We received a huge bonus from Oceane as well as one from her parents. We're in great shape."

"In that case, I should be able to stay home and heal."

"No. Because of the publicity, we have several new cases already, and Lix says the phones are ringing nonstop."

"Several new cases? Really? What's next?" Suddenly I felt as if I'd be ready for work by Monday after all. I had a feeling the new house and new girlfriend were both going to be mine for awhile.

"Lix gave me a synopsis of each while you were being treated. One in particular interests me. A man called Grant Munro wants not only our services as investigators into his husband's doings, but my advice on what he should do with his life as well."

"His husband?"

"Yes, they were among the first gay couples to be married in Vermont."

"What's the problem with his husband?"

"We'll have to see, won't we?" She knew she had me hooked. I'd been wishing for an easy case, maybe this was it. At least it wasn't murder.

ACKNOWLEDGMENTS

T HERE ARE SO MANY PEOPLE TO THANK. IF I'VE LEFT YOU out, it's because my mind is faulty, not because you don't deserve my appreciation. First, I thank my readers. Because you read *The Hounding*, or came to a reading, or were a beta reader for this book, you have encouraged me to continue this series. So you have no one to blame but yourselves if I write a book for every story A. Conan Doyle ever wrote about Sherlock Holmes.

Second, I am grateful to A. Conan Doyle who provided me with endless hours of entertainment both as a child and as an adult with his Sherlockian tales. And now of course, I've created my own female versions of SH and Dr. Watson. Watch for Moriarty in book three, *Valley of Fear*.

Third, a huge acknowledgment to my editor, Nann Dunne. She is the best. She knows editing (she studied it) and applies it with finesse. Nann helped me make this book the best it could be under my signature.

Fourth, I so appreciate my beta readers. They are the final "clean-up" crew for finding typos, grammatical errors, a glitch in continuity. Legal eagle eye Linda S. Pettit was especially on the ball, and Shirley A. King was the first to jump onboard, and gave me terrific feedback. Thank you so much.

Next, thank you to my many friends who follow me on Facebook, on Twitter, and who read my blog "Red Crested Chatter." Because of you, more people now know about Shirley Combs and Dr. Mary Watson.

Thank you to every person who bought my book, either in paperback or on Kindle. Thank you to the many people who downloaded my book on its free days and drove it up the Amazon ranks. Special thanks for those who borrowed the book through the Kindle library loan program, because that brings me royalties too. Thank you to those of you in other countries who bought my book because I feel so international when I deposit royalty checks from Germany, Italy, France, the UK, the Netherlands and Canada.

Finally, appreciation-in-print to my personal friends, family, and writing groups who have supported my writing for years. You know who you are.

What People Said about
The Hounding

I loved *The Hounding*. When is the next one coming out? An impatient reader.

From *Kirkus Review:* "A CONFIDENT, METICULOUSLY DETAILED mystery that would have made Shirley's pipe-smoking idol proud.

From reviewer Nancy Blackburn: "A comfortable lil' cozy, I felt that The Hounding was a really well written Indie book. Keep in mind that it is a cozy mystery, but it doesn't beat the reader over the head with the traditional definition of the "silly" cozy mystery! The book offered an excellent storyline, awesome twists and turns and wonderfully developed characters. Being a fan of Sherlock Holmes, I love to read 'plays' on his character and Ms. de Helen did a wonderful job!"

From customer Donna Spector: "THE PLOT IS COMPLEX, filled with red herring surprises and issues relevant to today's world. de Helen lets the suspense build to an astonishing and satisfying ending."

Coming Soon

A DARK THRILLER: *TILL DARKNESS COMES*, A NEW SERIES FEATURING a serial killer who preys on those who hurt others. The protagonist is Bess Vogelsang, a mixed race woman trying to put her difficult childhood behind her.

Follow Sandra de Helen's blog or Author page for updates re publications and author events. Her blog is Redcrested.com The author page is at Amazon.com/author/sandradehelen, and her website is SandradeHelen.com Follow her on Twitter @dehelen and on Facebook at http://on.fb.me/PUMt6o.

Till Darkness Comes

by Sandra de Helen

CHAPTER ONE:
SEMINAL EVENT

A SLIVER OF THE NEW MOON IS RISING THROUGH THE clouds as an unseen watcher leans closer to the closed window of the shed. The ramshackle building is covered in English ivy, honeysuckle, and a wild rambling rose that makes it difficult to see into the one-story wood working workshop that is lit with nothing but a Coleman lantern. Jerry Vogelsang sits on a stack of gunnysacks in his underwear, smoking, a can of Budweiser at his side. The boy is in a heap, wearing only his tee shirt, his back heaving with sobs.

"Get it together you little shit. You got to go inside and you got to act like everything's okay."

The boy jerks away from Jerry, but raises his head and faces him.

"Wipe your face and stuff. Straighten up."

The boy wipes his nose with the back of his hand, stands up, covering his private parts with his other hand. Jerry slaps the boy's hands away.

"Knock that off you little pussy. I already seen everything you got, and you seen mine. You liked it too, all right? Don't worry, I ain't gonna tell nobody. And you ain't either! You got it?" With that, Jerry grabs the boy's left ear and twists it until the boy drops to his knees, but the boy does not cry out.

"That's better. That's a little man. Now come here and let Uncle Jerry give you a kiss."

The boy steps forward and Jerry pulls the boy into his arms and kisses the boy on the mouth. Then he turns him around and gives him a push.

"Now get dressed and get in the house. Just act like you always do. Everything's okay. All right?"

"Okay."

With that, the boy scurries to put his clothes and shoes on, and runs out the door, letting it slam behind him. As soon as he is gone, the watcher goes around to the door, opens it, steps inside, and locks it.

Before Jerry can express more than surprise, the watcher crosses the room and knocks him in the head with a crowbar. That puts him out, and allows the watcher to prepare the room. First the window is covered with a black cloth. The door is barred to make it more secure than the lock by itself. Next the workbench is cleared to make room for Jerry. The watcher uses the firefighter's carry to get the thirty-seven-year-old onto the bench. He is of average height and weight, but he is unconscious, so of no help. Once he is on the table, the watcher secures him to it with ¾" galvanized metal strapping, using a nail gun. Jerry is strapped at neck, biceps, wrists, waist, thighs, knees, shins, and ankles. And one across the forehead for good measure. The watcher opens Jerry's mouth and stuffs it with a sock, then wraps a bandana around the back of his head and ties it over the sock in his mouth.

Jerry groans and begins to squirm. The watcher holds up a pair of scissors where Jerry can see them. He tries to yell and when he can't, he begins to thrash, his eyes wild. The scissors, held in hands encased in black rubber gloves, come at his face, stopping just short of his right eye. Jerry presses the back of his head into the workbench. Beads of sweat pop up on his forehead and a deep growl issues from his throat. The warm building reeks of bodily fluids.

"That's better. Now stay still just like that. I'm going to give you some shots so the things I do won't hurt so bad, okay? Shh. Be quiet now. You know we like to be quiet. We don't want anyone to know what you do out here in the shed, do we? No. So hold real still while I put this needle in your hand, and now the other one. Now I'm gonna cut your underpants off, here we go. Don't wiggle, you'll make me cut you. Woops, now see? I did cut you, these scissors are really sharp. Let's cut these all the way off, see what you've got down here. Well, that's not so much, is it? What's the matter, you cold? All the time I was thinking I'll bet you hurt that little boy you had in here, but maybe you didn't hurt him so bad with this little old thing here. Oh, but I'm forgetting. It gets hard when you're around little kids, right? Little boys and little girls both, right? You're equal like that, huh? A real man. Maybe you need to be a bit less of a man. Maybe you need to be castrated. Oh, don't worry, I'll give you some shots. Now hold still. Here we go. Are you numbing up yet? How about now? Look, it's not going to hurt that much anyway, right? I'm not going cut them off with the scissors. No. I'm going use dental floss. I'll tie them real tight and they will fall off in a couple of weeks. Hold still. Hold still!"

When Jerry continues to twist and turn, the metal banding starts to come loose. At the first sound of the nails pulling from the workbench, the watcher grabs the scissors and stabs Jerry in the stomach, then again higher in the chest, and finally in the throat. Blood is gushing from Jerry's body, but he is still. The watcher gathers up all the tools, including the black cloth from the window, the bar from the door, the crowbar, the nail gun, and what is left of the metal strapping. With a last look around, the watcher leaves the shed, shuts the door, pulls off the rubber gloves and stows them in a pocket.